CAST OF CHARACTERS

Five extraordinary siblings. One dangerous past. Unlimited potential.

Gretchen Wagner—The world-renowned cryptologist can crack any code, but her scrambled past—and the language of romance—still elude her. When a dark, seductive stranger offers to unlock the mysteries, will she like the answers she finds?

Kurt Miller—The steely private investigator has been hired to find Gretchen Wagner and bring her to her long-lost father. But could he be leading the woman who's trusted him with her heart into a deadly trap?

Jake Ingram—Now he knows the truth—that he's one of the Extraordinary Five (X5) children genetically engineered to possess superhuman abilities. And he knows what he has to do: find the others before a lethal enemy does!

Violet Vaughn Hobson—The birth mother of the X5, she's come out of hiding to save the children she thought were safe from a dangerous legacy.

About the Author

ANNE MARIE WINSTON

Writing a story about a woman who had no biological family or memory of anything before the age of twelve was the antithesis of Anne Marie Winston's own life, spent with a large extended family in a small town. Anne Marie sees family and friends weekly, walks where her beloved pets of yesteryear are laid to rest and has delightful memories of holding down the rock fort and making her own doll furniture with her cousins.

Anne Marie is a Pennsylvania native who began writing for Silhouette Books in 1991. Her family shares their home with eight dogs and cats, hosts a never-ending flow of teenage visitors and is raising a puppy for Guiding Eyes for the Blind. Anne Marie's writing career is studded with bestsellers and awards, most recently, the Golden Leaf in a Short Contemporary for her #1 bestseller from January 2001, *Billionaire Bachelors: Ryan*. To learn more about Anne Marie's novels, please visit her Web site at http://www.annemariewinston.com.

ANNE MARIE WINSTON

PYRAMID OF LIES

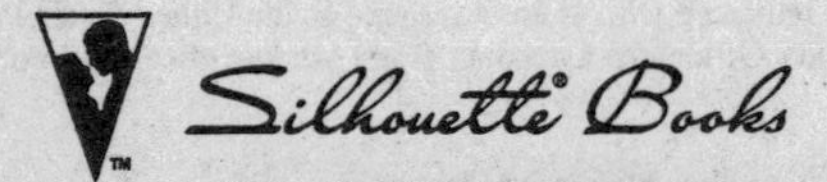

Published by Silhouette Books
America's Publisher of Contemporary Romance

Special thanks and acknowledgment are given to Anne Marie Winston for her contribution to the FAMILY SECRETS series.

ISBN 0-373-61369-5

PYRAMID OF LIES

This edition published by arrangement with Harlequin Books S.A.

Visit us at www.silhouettefamilysecrets.com

Printed in U.S.A.

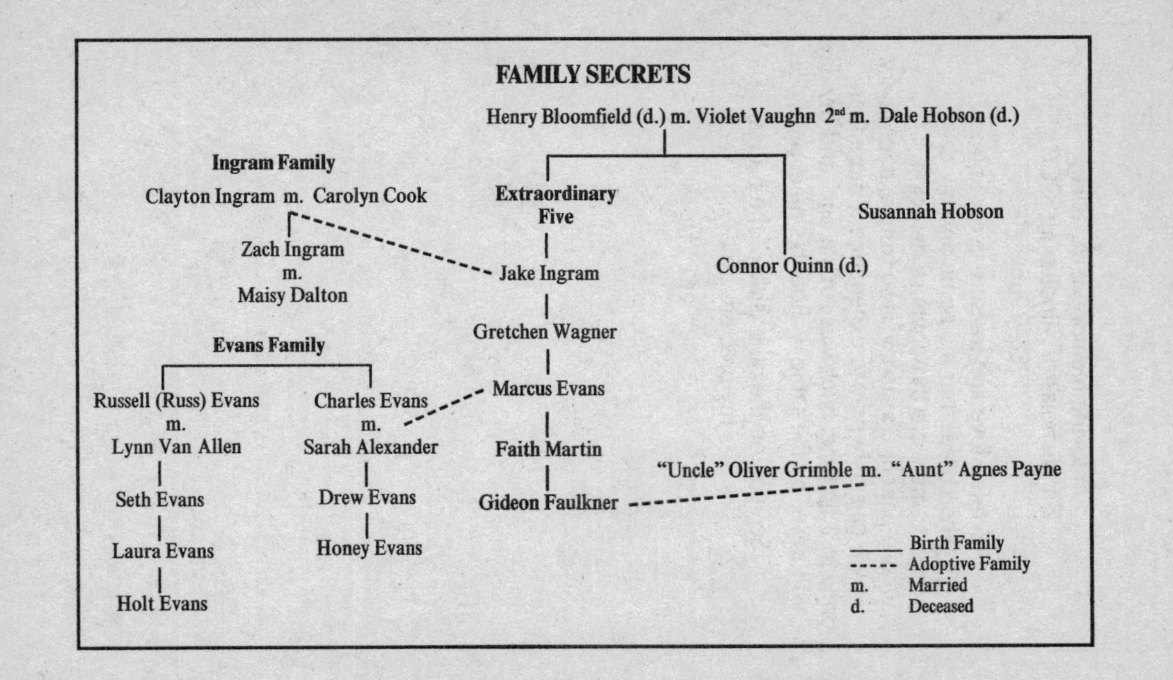
FAMILY SECRETS
Henry Bloomfield (d.) m. Violet Vaughn 2nd m. Dale Hobson (d.)
Extraordinary Five
Connor Quinn (d.)
Susannah Hobson
Jake Ingram
Gretchen Wagner
Marcus Evans
Faith Martin
Gideon Faulkner
Ingram Family
Clayton Ingram m. Carolyn Cook
Zach Ingram
m.
Maisy Dalton
Evans Family
Russell (Russ) Evans
m.
Lynn Van Allen
Seth Evans
Laura Evans
Holt Evans
Charles Evans
m.
Sarah Alexander
Drew Evans
Honey Evans
"Uncle" Oliver Grimble m. "Aunt" Agnes Payne
Birth Family
Adoptive Family
m. Married
d. Deceased

In loving memory of my Nick,
Sir Nicholas of Middleburg, CGC
1988–2002

While I love and treasure every animal
who comes into my home and my care,
there are those whose devotion,
whose patient constancy, is so truly extraordinary,
we can only pray to experience it more than
once in a lifetime. Nick was such a one, and my days
will never be the same without his quiet presence.

See you on the other side of the bridge,
my precious boy.

One

''Uh-oh. I see that look in your eye.''

''What look?'' Gretchen Wagner barely heard her assistant's teasing tone. She was too busy watching an infant with enormous dark eyes who was securely nestled in the curve of his mother's arm. The mother, she noted, wore Western dress and looked a good deal cooler than Gretchen and Nancy. Even in the May desert heat, they each wore an ankle-length dress and a linen scarf wrapped loosely around their heads in deference to Egyptian modesties.

The two women passed through the heavy glass doors that fronted their Cairo hotel and entered the deep chill of the lobby. Both of them unwrapped their *hijabs* from around their heads and necks, automatically pausing as they folded the lengths of gauzy fabric.

''That maternal, googly-eyed, 'isn't-he-sweet' look. Are you getting the urge to nest?'' Nancy Claxten didn't sound particularly enthusiastic, and Gretchen slanted her research assistant a questioning look as she avoided the question.

''Don't you like children?'' she asked. It was inconceivable to her that anyone could fail to be enthralled by a helpless infant.

"They're okay." Nancy shrugged. "It's not that I don't like them. It's more where I am in my life, you know?"

Gretchen didn't know. Her childhood was a blank slate, courtesy of some trauma, the psychologists assumed, that had occurred during her twelfth year when she'd been adopted by Hans and Annika Wagner. She'd never had friends like most kids, at least not that she remembered, and by the time she'd been adopted, she'd been so different that she'd had no hope of figuring out the complex nuances that comprised teenage interaction.

Friends were a luxury for kids who fit in during adolescence. For those who didn't... It hadn't mattered much to her, anyway, since she'd been so advanced in her studies that she'd been accelerated in school and had graduated at fifteen. At twenty she'd finished both her B.A. and her Masters in Linguistics. Her doctorate in Ancient World Writings and Transliteration at the tender age of twenty-two had been followed shortly thereafter with the first of several prestigious positions at acclaimed universities across the country. She spoke and read eleven living languages, had a solid acquaintance with several others and could read Latin and Greek.

But she'd never been anywhere near a baby in her entire adult life.

So no, she didn't know what Nancy meant. And

she wouldn't have cared until a few months ago, when she'd realized her biological clock was ringing a strident alarm, warning her to get on the procreation bandwagon before it left her behind.

"Where are you in your life?" she asked Nancy.

"Too young to want to be tied down. Besides, I'm the oldest of six kids. I've done enough baby-sitting to satisfy me for a long, long time." Nancy grinned at Gretchen. "Besides, I'm only twenty-two."

Lucky girl. She had plenty of years ahead of her. All those eggs in her ovaries were in prime condition.

"You, on the other hand," Nancy went on, "probably don't want to fool around too much longer to snag a man and get started if you want a family. You're about forty, right?"

"Mid-thirties," Gretchen hedged. Did she look that bad?

"Oops. I was about to tell you that you didn't look nearly that old. Swear to God. My mother just turned forty but believe me, she looks like she's on the downhill side of the decade. You barely look thirty. My mom's youngest sister is thirty and she looks like hell compared to you. Of course, she's got three kids. Maybe the stress of screwing up your face in childbirth makes your skin start to sag faster or—"

"Stop it." Gretchen was doing her best not to laugh. "You're just making it worse."

"Making what worse?" Nancy looked genuinely puzzled.

"This whole baby thing." Gretchen spread a hand

before her in an uncharacteristically expansive gesture and took a deep breath. She'd never confided her desire for a family of her own to anyone before. "Your thirty-year-old aunt has three children. See? I'm a relic. On the shelf. I'll never have a family."

"Jeez." Nancy rolled her eyes. "Half of it's your fault, you know. You don't make much of an effort."

"I beg your pardon?" She didn't know what response she'd expected, but that was hardly it.

"Granted, the guys in the academic world are total geeks, but you barely bother to acknowledge them unless you need to discuss research. How are you going to meet your studly prince if you don't talk to him first?"

It was hard to take offense when the younger woman was so matter-of-factly sincere. "Since when have you seen a studly prince in the hallways of University College London?"

"You have a good point." Nancy skirted the edge of a group of chairs as they crossed the marble floor. "Studs are few and far between at UCL. Dr. Wagner, you've got to broaden your horizons if you want to find a man."

"Actually," Gretchen said, "I've been thinking about this for a while. I don't really want to find a man."

"You're gay? Sorry I was pushing the whole straight scene—"

"No, I'm not gay!" Her voice might have been a little louder than she'd intended, causing a ruggedly handsome dark-haired man sitting in one of the lobby's elegant chairs to look up, clearly startled. She lowered her voice, her face burning. "I just meant that I'm perfectly able to conceive and bear a child today without involving a man."

"You mean in vitro, sperm bank, that kind of deal?" Nancy raised her eyebrows doubtfully as they reached the bank of elevators. "Doesn't that cost a fortune? And also, do you really want to be a single parent? That would totally suck in my book. Who would get the kid out of your hair when you're having major PMS? Or what if you got the flu? Or—"

"Nancy." Gretchen kept her tone measured. "Do you know the meaning of the phrase 'wet blanket'?"

"Sure, I— Oh." Nancy smiled wryly. "Gotcha."

A bell dinged and the elevator doors slid open. After Gretchen and Nancy entered, the dark-haired man from the lobby stepped on behind them. He met Gretchen's gaze briefly and smiled slightly as he stepped to the panel and checked the buttons they'd already pressed. It was a pleasant smile, not a smug one, but she was still appalled that he'd overheard part of the admittedly bizarre conversation. Apparently he was on the same floor one of them was, because he settled back without punching any additional buttons.

In the silence of the elevator Gretchen risked a second glance at the stranger. He was a very handsome man, with wavy brown hair cut short and practical, and dark brown, long-lashed eyes. Although he was deeply tanned, he clearly wasn't from the Middle East, but of Anglo-Saxon extraction. He had a square, stubborn jaw, and the creases in his cheeks became deep dimples when he smiled. And he was big. Not extraordinarily tall, although probably around six feet, but burly. His shoulders and arms were defined and hard-looking, like those of a man who kept himself in top physical condition with weight-training. When he crossed his arms over his chest, the short-sleeved polo shirt he wore strained at the seams.

Then Nancy cleared her throat and when Gretchen looked her way, the younger woman grinned and waggled her eyebrows.

Gretchen narrowed her eyes and Nancy's smile widened before she spoke. "I'm going over to Pub 28 with some of the other research assistants tonight. We're going to grab a bite to eat first. You should join us. Your prince might be out there somewhere."

Good grief. Would there be anything worse than going to a bar full of ex-pats on the prowl with a bunch of students who would make her feel older than Methuselah? Especially with Nancy envisioning herself in the role of matchmaker? Besides, Nancy knew she didn't fraternize with her students. Heck, she didn't fraternize with anybody.

"No, thanks," she said, although she tried to soften her refusal. Nancy was an excellent assistant and probably the closest thing Gretchen had ever had to a real friend. They'd met at Harvard when Nancy had taken several of her courses and the girl had jumped at the offer to accompany Gretchen to Egypt to work on the Ahkramihton Tablets project. Nancy was incapable of working silently and Gretchen had found herself letting down the ingrained barriers she normally hid behind. "The heat down here is getting to me. I'm going to have a quiet meal in the hotel and get a good night's sleep. But thanks anyway."

"No problem. But remember what I said about broadening your horizons." Nancy paused as the elevator doors opened at her floor, but when she didn't get any response, she shrugged and waved as she stepped out of the car. "Shall I meet you in the lobby at nine again?"

Gretchen nodded. "Sure. Have a good evening."

"You, too."

The elevator doors slid closed on her young assistant, leaving Gretchen and the gorgeous stranger alone in the little car.

She looked at the floor, embarrassed as she recalled what Nancy had said about her prince. Great. So now the attractive man thought she was one of those desperate single women looking for the right man under every rock—or in every bar. She could feel heat climbing into her cheeks and she glanced up at the numbers above the door. One floor to go.

The man cleared his throat and she glanced at him. Oh, Lord, he was looking at her. "You're American?" He was clearly from the States, with a definite drawl hinting at a past in the South. His voice was deep and slightly husky, exactly the kind of voice she'd have expected to go with that face. Which never happened. In her experience, which was laughably limited, when a man looked totally hot, he had a squeaky tone or sounded nasal or had some other grating vocal quality that made for a jarring surprise that dampened a woman's interest. Okay, dampened *her* interest. She could hardly speak for other women.

She nodded. Then, realizing that seemed curt, she said, "Yes." Rats. That sounded curt, too. As Nancy so elegantly would have put it, she sucked at small talk. In fact, she sucked at pretty much anything to do with men.

"I thought so. It's nice to hear another American accent."

"Even if it isn't from the South?"

The man laughed. His eyes crinkled at the corners. "Even if it isn't from Texas."

The elevator bell dinged and the doors slid smoothly open. She stepped off, aware that the stranger was close behind her. Her room was the first on the left when she turned the corner from the elevator foyer, and the good-looking stranger detoured around her as he strode on down the hall.

"Have a nice evening," he said, smiling at her again.

Gretchen glanced at him from beneath her lashes, too tongue-tied to do more than mumble, "Thank you."

In her room, she stripped off the practical blouse and long khaki skirt she'd worn. She wasn't used to the dry heat in this part of the world and her skin felt as if every particle of moisture had been leached from it. After adding a generous amount of her favorite scented bath beads to a tepid bath, she pinned up her hair and soaked in the pleasantly cool water until her fingertips began to wrinkle. After the bath, she smoothed lotion onto every inch of her body, sighing with pleasure as her dry skin drank in the cream.

An hour later, she put on a lightweight loose dress that fell from an empire waist in tiny pleats to the floor, draped a shawl around her shoulders and went down to dinner. She'd been to Egypt and other parts of the Middle East several times before and had an effectively modest wardrobe specifically for such trips. A woman on her own couldn't be too careful, especially in this part of the world where the Islamic religion and culture were intricately intertwined.

There were several restaurants in the hotel that catered to its international guests. There were three small cafés with different ethnic foods, a large and formal restaurant with servers in tuxedos, and an equally large but far more intimate place that served American cuisine, as well as two bars that served sandwiches. She chose the American place and was promptly seated at a small table.

It was in a little alcove rather than out in the middle of the room and for that she was grateful. Although she was used to eating alone and had done it for much of her adult life, she always hated it. She was positive everyone else in the restaurant saw her and pitied the poor woman who didn't have a dinner companion.

Gretchen, you are truly pathetic. Stop being so self-absorbed.

Be as self-absorbed as you like, said another inner voice. *If you don't treat yourself well, who will?*

With that exchange rattling around in her brain, she boldly ordered a nice Pinot Grigio to go with her meal.

It wasn't often that she felt as restless and edgy as she felt tonight, and she wasn't really sure why she did. Maybe it had something to do with finishing up her project. When her scholarly study on the Ahkramihton Tablets was published, it was going to make a definite splash worldwide. A short-lived splash, to anyone outside the community that studied the ancient world, perhaps, but still a splash. The Ahk Tablets, as they were commonly known, contained what was undeniably the earliest writing ever done by man, dating back at least five hundred years before Sumerian protocuneiform or the hieroglyphics of ancient Egypt.

As the world's leading expert in ancient writings, Gretchen had been retained to decipher the previously unknown script that had never been seen before. Today she'd unraveled the last two characters that had eluded her. The tablets could be interpreted now. So she did, indeed, have something to celebrate. It was undoubtedly the most important work she'd ever done, the pinnacle of her career. And yet…it wasn't enough.

Her morose reflections of a moment earlier pointed out the holes in her success as clearly as black ink on white parchment. She might be an academic success, her name might always be remembered for contributing to the body of work on the Ahkramihton Tablets, but she had no one to share it with. No one who would care one way or another if she dropped off the planet tomorrow.

She was a big fat failure in the relationship arena. And she strongly suspected that it was far too late to alter her destiny in that regard. There was, however, one thing she could do that would change her life completely, that would mean she would never be truly alone again.

She could have a baby.

A baby! The thought had been prodding its way out of her subconscious mind for a while now, she realized. Fueled by encounters with fat, happy infants and serene-faced mothers, encouraged by her conversation with Nancy today, the notion of becoming a mother had taken root in her mind and slowly grown, just like a fertilized egg in a womb. A private smile curved her mouth upward at the corners and she took another sip of her wine in a silent toast to herself. It was easily the most radical thing she'd ever considered, but the more she thought it through, the better an idea it seemed. A child of her own, a child with half her biological material making up its cells, not an adopted child. Though there was nothing wrong with adopting, she admonished herself hastily. Thank God for people like her own parents, who wanted a child no matter whose it had been before. And she'd do that, of course, if it were her only option. But…

She didn't want to go through the next half of her life alone. And if she had a child of her own, she would finally have that biological connection she'd always craved. She'd never said anything about it while her parents were alive. Indeed, she hadn't even let herself think about it back then, because she would have died before hurting them. But with each year that passed, the urge to bear a biological descendant had grown stronger.

It wasn't just biology. It was the *connection* she craved. She wanted a second chance, a chance to give a child all the things she couldn't remember having. A child whose birthday would always be celebrated on the date of his birth every year, a child who had photographs and videos, parental anecdotes and memories from his very earliest moments on earth.

Picking up her wineglass, she silently toasted herself. Just as soon as she got back to Boston, she was going to begin searching for a man to father her child. Sex with a strange man solely for the purpose of procreating wasn't exactly the most appealing thought, but she didn't really have a choice. Artificial insemination and in vitro fertilization were costly procedures, she'd read, and although she lived well, she didn't have a lot of extra cash to throw around, particularly if she was going to become a mother. She'd need to save every penny in that case.

Her parents had been wealthy but she'd given most of her inheritance away years ago. She'd been satisfied with her life and her work and, she'd reasoned, more good could be done in her parents' memory that way than it could sitting in her investment accounts.

But now...now she wished that she'd kept just a few hundred thousand for a rainy day. Oh, well, she hadn't and that was that. So she'd be procreating the old-fashioned way. A nervous giggle erupted before she could discipline herself. Lord, she'd better get a grip. What would she be like with a man if just thinking about it made her nervous?

She didn't look around at the other diners to see if anyone was watching her bizarre behavior. They wouldn't be. She was the original invisible woman.

Oh, well. She gave a mental shrug. It wasn't as if she minded it. Being nondescript was an asset in many ways. A forgettable person didn't attract undue attention, which she loathed with a passion. She nearly smiled, remembering how her mother had tried to interest her in dance lessons or the drama club. Even organized sports filled Gretchen with dread—all those spectators watching her, waiting for her to make a mistake.

That, she thought, was another one of the reasons she wanted a child of her own. Her baby wasn't going to have to be perfect. She'd love it anyway.

She clenched her fist on her fork so hard the metal edge dug into her slender fingers. Why did she feel like that? Her parents hadn't pressured her. They'd only wanted to be sure she had any opportunities she cared to try. If only she could remember what her life had been like for the first twelve years of her existence. It was enough to drive a person crazy!

God knew, she didn't have anything else in her life to get worked up about. Or any one. Since her parents had both passed away, she'd buried herself in work to avoid acknowledging how isolated she felt.

She didn't even know her true birthdate. How pathetic was that?

Her adoptive parents had celebrated her birthday on Valentine's Day, saying they had gotten their heart's desire the day they adopted Gretchen, but after their respective deaths she'd found her adoption papers. Except for the year, 1967, the actual date had been left blank, as had any reference to her biological parents. It was almost as if she had never existed before the day they'd brought her home. Which she knew couldn't be true.

She'd had a dozen years of a life before her adoption. For some reason that no doctor had ever been able to discern, her memory of her childhood before that point was limited to a hazy image of a pretty dark-haired woman—her mother?—and a wide stretch of sandy beach with gentle waves that frothed onto the shore in endlessly mesmerizing, rolling breakers.

Those memories had been with her always, and she generally dismissed them. Her adoption had been private and there were no records left to peruse even if she had wanted to find her birth parents. Which she didn't. After more than two decades, what would be the point? Obviously, her memory loss was from some physical or emotional trauma stemming from a childhood spent with those parents. The beach...who knew? A vacation memory, perhaps? For Gretchen, the bottom line was that she'd been adopted by two warm, gentle people who made her feel safe and loved. What would be the point in subjecting herself to possibly years of therapy to try to recover memories that might be better left buried?

She began to read the menu the server had handed her, and as she did so, a shadow fell across her table.

"Good evening."

That voice! She felt a tingle of instant recognition as she looked up. It was, as she'd known, the stranger from the elevator. In the next second she recalled her comment about not being gay that he'd overheard and she immediately began to blush furiously.

He didn't appear to notice. "Are you waiting for someone?"

She shook her head and cleared her throat. "Ah, no."

The man smiled and extended his hand. "I'm Kurt Miller. From Austin, Texas. May I join you for dinner?"

Two

Violet Vaughn Hobson paced nervously around the spacious suite of rooms at the Wardman Park Marriott in Washington, D.C. Two minutes past six.

He wasn't coming. She knew it. And really, she couldn't blame the boy. He surely thought this whole thing was a hoax.

The *man,* she reminded herself. Jake was a grown man now. For more than two decades she'd held in her head the image of the wary boy he'd been the last time she'd seen him…it had been a shock to see how tall he'd grown, how broad his shoulders were. For one heartbreaking instant she'd seen his father Henry in the set of those shoulders. And then his gaze had lit on her and she'd seen the same blue eyes she knew so well from looking into her own mirror every morning.

A sharp knock on the door jolted her. Pressing a hand to her racing heart, she walked to the door and checked to see who her visitor was. Relief so strong it nearly buckled her knees rushed through her as she saw the dear face of her oldest son staring back at her through the peephole. Taking a deep, fortifying breath, she placed her hand on the knob and pulled open the heavy hotel door.

"Hello, Jake." She propped her slender body against the door to hold it open and held out her right hand in greeting. "I'm Violet—Vi—Hobson. I'm your biological mother."

Jake Ingram reached out, automatically taking her hand, but a moment later she saw the full import of her words sink in, and he froze, letting her hand slide from his. He rallied almost immediately, stepping into the room as he turned to a second man she hadn't noticed before and said, "Do you mind waiting outside, Robert?"

"I'll stay right here," a deep voice answered.

"Who's that?" she asked, startled.

"Bodyguard." He gave no further explanation as he closed the door. As he turned and looked at her again, she almost felt the skepticism that instantly filled the space between them. "Pardon me if I find your claim hard to credit," he said, "but I thought I was an orphan. Why should I believe you?"

Violet motioned to the large, elegant sitting room behind her. He might not want to believe her, but she'd seen the flicker of uncertainty in his eyes. Uncertainty, no doubt from the notes she'd sent him earlier telling him that she knew the truth about his past. She thought, too, of the recent spate of frantic rumors about genetically engineered children that the media had been spewing since the government had accidentally declassified the Medusa papers. Did he suspect that he could be one of them? With his extraordinary intellectual abilities, the notion surely had to have crossed his mind. She didn't mention that either, instead simply said, "I led your adoptive family to that conclusion for a very good reason. If you'd like to come in, I'd be happy to explain."

Mistrust narrowed his eyes. She couldn't blame him. "I know about your...brother," she said. "Zachary. I believe he was kidnapped because he was thought to be you." Jake didn't seem surprised or shocked, and as she realized that had already occurred to him, the reason for the bodyguard became clear. Relief washed through her. "You've been taking security precautions since then, haven't you?"

He nodded, eyes watchful. "Anyone could claim to know about the kidnapping, since we plastered the media with reward information in exchange for anything that led to an arrest."

"Actually, I first saw it in the newspaper," she said. "That's how I recognized you." Her voice quavered despite her best efforts. "Except for the eyes, you look so much like your father."

His expression didn't change. "Why do you think I was the target of the kidnapping?"

She could practically see his analytical mind at work. She sighed as she indicated the living room and walked toward a grouping of seats. "You're valuable," she said bluntly, sensing his need to get to the heart of it. "It's a long story and I'll try to keep it brief. But there are several things you must know. First, you have brothers and sisters. All adopted as older children like yourself and I'm afraid you're all in danger—''

''Why don't I remember them? Or you?'' His voice was challenging; she could practically see the aggression roiling around inside him.

''Your memories were suppressed by unethical people,'' she said, striving for calm. Acting like a raving maniac would only confirm any fears he already had about her sanity. ''I tried to get help for you, but there wasn't much that could be done—''

''Did we live near the beach?''

''Yes!'' She felt a disproportionate thrill at this sign that perhaps he *did* remember. ''Do you remember anything else?''

''Very little. Other than the fact that you think I look like someone you know, why do you think I'm your son?''

''Knew,'' she corrected softly. ''Your father is dead. But beyond the physical similarities, there are your abilities—'' She halted as he made an abrupt movement, terrified that he was about to terminate the meeting, but he only settled himself on his chair. ''I'd better start at the beginning.''

''Please do.'' It wasn't a request. Her son had matured into a leader, a decision-maker, just as he'd been when he'd been a young boy at play with his siblings. Pride surged through her. They might have taken her children away, might have altered their memories, but they hadn't been able to damage the inner core that made them who they were. At least, that was what she prayed.

She took another deep breath. ''Your father was Dr. Henry Bloomfield. He was one of the earliest researchers in the field of genetic engineering.'' Jake recoiled noticeably at those words, but she forged ahead. ''He was a brilliant man. Emory University initially funded his research, which was called Code Proteus. But in 1966, our grant was cut from the budget. Henry was livid.'' She winced at the memory, smiling wryly. ''He didn't get worked up about much, but *that* news set him off like nothing I'd ever seen.''

''Where did you meet? Were you married then?''

Violet sobered. There was so much to explain...and no time for all of it. ''I was his lab assistant. But that can wait.'' Agitated, she stood and walked to the marble mantel. ''Henry was determined to carry on with Code Proteus. So he got in touch with a special wing of the CIA known as Medusa, who had been trying to recruit him for years. Medusa agreed to fund the project, so Henry moved the whole operation south to his family home in Belle Terre, North Carolina. It was a beautiful oceanfront home.''

She stopped, gauging Jake's reaction again. He appeared to be taking her story in stride so far. But that had been the easy part. ''By 1967, Henry had perfected his research and a number of eggs were successfully fertilized and implanted. It's commonplace technology now, but in 1967,'' she heard the ring of pride in her own voice, "it was unheard of. I was both the egg donor and the surrogate mother. Henry was the sperm donor. In November of 1967, you were born, along with a sister and a brother. All fraternal, all genetically engineered for certain superior qualities."

"Genetically engineered," Jake repeated. "Are you trying to tell me that my facility for numbers, my intellect, wasn't just some stroke of lucky biology?"

Violet shook her head. "No." Then a sudden surge of grief welled up and she turned her back, resting her forehead against the cool marble. God, it had been over thirty years and she still could hardly bear to think about her second-born son. She swallowed, waiting until she thought she could speak without sobbing. "Your brother died at birth."

There was a silence behind her. "And the girl?"

"Your sister's name is Grace. *Was* Grace. It might have been changed when she was adopted." She straightened and turned around. "She looks—" She uttered a broken laugh. "She looks a lot like me. At least, she did when she was twelve. I can't believe she'd have changed so terribly much."

"And what does she do?"

"I don't know. I haven't been able to locate her yet."

"No." His tone was impatient. "What kind of special...talents does she have? Are we all numbers geeks?"

"Oh, no." She could answer that. "Grace was tremendously skilled with languages. She could decode anything I could throw at her. And by the time she was ten, she spoke fluent English, Spanish, French, Japanese and Italian."

Jake stood. Skepticism chased itself across his face. "This is nuts," he muttered, half to himself. Absently, he lifted one hand and plunged his fingers into his thick dark hair, dragging it back from his forehead.

Violet felt her heart knock violently against her ribs as the gesture sent a bittersweet arrow of loving memory straight through her. "Your father did that," she whispered. "Just exactly like that."

"What?" Jake looked at her as if she'd gone crazy. "Did what?"

"That hair thing." She demonstrated, yanking her own still-dark hair up and away from her forehead just as he had.

Jake was watching her and suddenly she saw his eyes widen. His pupils went dark with shock and he put a hand on the back of a nearby wing chair. "Jake?" She felt panic rise. "What is it? Are you ill?"

He dropped his head and shook it slowly from side to side. "No. Not ill." His voice sounded dazed, very different from the self-assured man who'd entered the room a short time ago. Then he lifted his head. He took three steps to her side, and she nearly backed away as he lifted a hand to her forehead and brushed aside her hair.

"You have the scar," he said in a low, wondering voice. "All these years, that's one of the few memories I've had, just this vague impression of my mother having a 'boo-boo' right there." He chuckled a little at the childish term but he was clearly shaken. His blue eyes met hers, and she was overwhelmed by the emotion in the bottomless wells. "I remember…I remember my mother being in bed. For a long time."

She nodded, nearly undone by the feel of her son's fingers gently tracing her scar. "I fell down the stairs and broke my ankle. But part of the reason I had to stay in bed was because I was pregnant again. You have two more younger brothers and a sister."

Gretchen simply stared at Kurt Miller. When he smiled, he was devastating. His brown eyes crinkled at the corners and glinted with warm humor, and the dimples in his cheeks deepened. His teeth were white and even, drawing her gaze to his mouth, and she felt a ball of pure panic lodge in her stomach.

"I, uh… You don't know anything about me. Why would you want to have dinner with me?"

"I know you're American. I know you're not gay." His smile made the statement a joke, rather than a come-on. "I know your friend wants you to broaden your horizons and that you're meeting her tomorrow at nine." He reached into an inner pocket of his jacket and withdrew a business card, extending it to her. "Say yes," he urged. "I'm harmless and more homesick than ever since I heard your accent in the elevator. I thought it would be nice to share a meal with a fellow countryman. And you can tell your friend how broad your horizons are becoming."

To give herself time, she examined the card. *Kurt J. Miller, Licensed Private Investigator. Discreet. Efficient.*

He was more appealing than any man should be, and she hoped he wasn't a con artist or a crazed killer, because he was so attractive she couldn't resist the chance to spend a little time with him.

Kurt Miller was tall and solidly built as she'd noted in the elevator, with broad shoulders and tanned arms like polished teak where they extended from the short sleeves of his lightweight dress shirt. His eyes, each time she met his gaze, were warm, and she felt an astonishing tug of instant attraction. Astonishing because she rarely noticed men, and when she did, they certainly never returned the interest. This man was looking at her almost...admiringly!

"I, uh... That would be nice," she said hastily. Then, feeling like a complete clod, she indicated the chair across from her own. "Please, sit down."

As he pulled out the chair with large, capable-looking hands, she placed the card in her purse. She was mildly astounded at herself. She'd never done anything like this in her whole life!

So maybe it was time she did.

"You know my name, it's only fair to tell me yours," he said.

"Oh, sorry." She winced, sure he was thinking what a bozo she was. "Gretchen Wagner. I'm from Boston."

"Boston. I've never been to Boston. Did you grow up there?"

She shook her head. "No, my parents were from Phoenix. But I'm on the faculty at Harvard."

His eyebrows rose and he whistled. "Harvard. What do you teach?"

"Ancient writings." She made a face. "I know, it sounds dry and boring. And it probably is to anyone who doesn't have an interest in history and the development of language."

"It doesn't sound boring at all," he assured her. "Are you in Egypt to study hieroglyphics?"

She nearly smiled. Early Egypt's hieroglyphics were child's play compared to what she was doing now. "No," she merely said. "My interest lies in a different form of writing recently discovered. It's actually centuries older than the first hieroglyphics."

She thought back to two years ago, when she'd first been retained by the University of Cairo to decipher the seventeen Ahk Tablets that had been found in a newly excavated city site that predated anything yet discovered. Similar in composition to Sumerian protocuneiform, the tablets were filled with meticulous characters. Unfortunately, though they bore a resemblance to cuneiform, they were of no written language so far known to modern man.

That's when Gretchen had been called. Because of the prestige such work would bring to the university, Harvard was all too happy to give her a sabbatical to pursue the research.

She'd quickly realized what a treasure the find was. Since then, with an additional grant underwritten by the National Geographic Society, she'd spent the past twenty-four months, first at Harvard, then at University College London and now in Cairo, working to document and decipher the script, which turned out to be significantly more complex linguistically than cuneiform. As the project neared completion, she'd returned to Cairo for final comparisons between her work and the actual tablets. She was nearly finished now, and she could almost taste the satisfaction she felt at sharing the legacy of a long-dead culture with the world.

National Geographic had featured her progress on their Web site for months now. They'd done one early piece in the monthly magazine and in the current issue had published a second update on her progress. She envisioned the spread that would reveal her ultimate findings and which would make her work available to the layman rather than just the dry academics.

"What brings you to Egypt?" she asked. She wasn't eager to discuss her work further. It would only make her look like a supergeek to the gorgeous man across the table.

Kurt caught the waiter's eye and motioned the man over. After he'd placed his drink order, he said, "Actually, I'm combining business with pleasure. I'm a private investigator and I needed to come to Cairo in regard to a case I'm working on, so I decided to turn it into a little vacation while I was here. The Middle East is so unstable I'd probably never choose to come here by design, but since I'm here, I plan to take the opportunity to see the pyramids and some of the other tourist attractions. It's incredibly humbling to see structures and artifacts that were crafted so long ago."

His tone was genuinely reverent, and Gretchen felt herself relaxing a little. She felt much the same. The server returned with Kurt's drink and took their dinner orders before quietly fading away. For a moment, there was a small, awkward silence.

"Tell me more about your work," he said. "It sounds fascinating."

She couldn't prevent a wry smile. "Not everyone would agree with you. But I enjoy it enormously."

She went on to explain more about the Ahk Tablets to him, answering his questions with rising delight. He actually seemed interested in the type of work she did. They ate as they talked until finally the server cleared the table and brought Kurt the brandy he'd requested. She nursed a cup of decaf tea, declining alcohol.

"Do you have a family back in Texas?" Realizing that they'd spoken almost exclusively about her, she seized on the earlier comment he'd made about being homesick.

A shadow of regret, or perhaps, sadness, flickered across his strong features. "Not anymore," he said, slowly turning his drink glass, gazing at the patterns the liquid made. "My grandmother raised me and she's gone now."

"Why did your grandmother raise you?" It didn't occur to her that the question was far too personal, and probably rude, until she saw his eyebrows quirk up. "I'm sorry," she began. "That's none of my business."

"I don't mind," he said mildly. "My parents were killed when I was young. I barely remember them."

"I don't remember my parents, either. My birth parents," she told him. "I'm adopted."

His eyebrows rose. "So we have something in common." He smiled slowly at her and the moment held, lingered as the rest of the evening sounds in the restaurant faded away and the world shrank until there was nothing but the two of them, his gaze holding hers. Her stomach jittered and the breath she took was shallow and uneven. Kurt's smile slowly faded, and when he spoke again, his voice was low and rough. "Will you have dinner with me again tomorrow evening?"

Jake closed his eyes briefly, shook his head again. "This is too much to take in." He exhaled heavily, then returned to sit on the edge of a wing chair with his hands hanging loosely between his knees. Violet sensed it was an uncharacteristically indecisive pose for him. ''Let's back up a minute,'' he said. ''You said Zach was kidnapped because I'm valuable?'' He snorted. ''Okay. Let's not beat around the bush. I know exactly how smart I am. But Zach's pretty damned smart, too. Why would the kidnappers want me so much? At first, Zach and I assumed they wanted to block the World Bank Heist investigation by killing me, but that doesn't really fit. They certainly didn't have to kidnap me if all they wanted was to kill me.''

''It really has nothing to do with the World Bank incident,'' she told him. ''It has to do with a certain unsavory group of people getting their hands on you and your brothers and sisters again. I suspect the robbery was simply to finance their work.''

''Again?'' His eyebrows rose.

''They killed your father.'' Her voice was flat as she recited the devastating events of over twenty years before. ''Then they tried to take you from me. They suppressed your memories—when I got away and stole you all back, you didn't even remember me. I managed to save you by making everyone believe we all died. Until recently I was successful.''

''But I've been in the news,'' he finished wryly.

Violet nodded. ''Yes. I'm quite certain they realize you're alive now. I recognized you by your particular intellectual skills, but when I saw a picture of you, that confirmed it. You're almost a dead ringer for Henry, and several of the people I believe are involved knew him quite well. It's a sure bet they've identified you as well. Zach was kidnapped mistakenly."

"So who's 'they'? Who's behind this?" She could almost see that lightning-fast intellect sorting and processing the new information.

"I suspect it's my former co-workers," she said. "Some or all of them, I don't know. And they must have had funding, assistance, through the years."

"There were at least three people involved in Zach's kidnapping," he said. "He said a younger man—who was killed—reported to an older couple, a man and woman named Agnes and Oliver." His eyes darkened. "I'm pretty sure I met them at a social event a few months ago. They must have been after me even then."

Violet shivered convulsively as a chill raced down her spine and dread coalesced into frightening certainty. *Agnes and Oliver.* And she'd bet her very last nickel that Croft was involved as well.

"Who the hell are they?" Jake sounded impatient and she couldn't blame him. This was a tremendously complicated mess.

"Agnes Payne and Oliver Grimble. The two scientists who once worked with your father and me on Code Proteus. They helped raise you and the others but Henry and I feared they had other plans for you.

I don't know who the younger person would have been—maybe hired help?—but I think there might be another man involved, a former Medusa agent named Willard Croft.''

''And these three want me?''

''Yes.'' She was becoming more certain by the moment.

''And Grace and the others,'' Jake surmised. ''But why? What could they hope to gain with us? So what if each of us is extraordinarily intelligent and gifted in certain fields?''

''That alone could be enough if you could be forced to work for them,'' she said. ''But there's more. The night we escaped, one of your brothers was caught. They shot him and I thought...I thought he had died.'' Her voice hitched as she remembered the horror and despair she'd felt when she'd thought Gideon was dead. ''But he's alive. He was involved in the bank robbery.''

Jake was stunned. ''My own brother? Are you sure?''

Violet twisted her fingers together in agitation. ''They're controlling him. I'm certain of it. And I'm afraid they want to do the same thing with all of you. Think, Jake, of the damage a biologist who understands viruses could do. Or a computer expert who could disrupt systems worldwide.''

Her son actually paled. ''We have to get to them first.''

She nodded. ''Exactly.''

"Who are they? And *where* are they?"

She grimaced, wishing she had more for him. "I wish I knew. I haven't had time to locate any of them. All I know are their birth names, the cities in which their adoptions occurred and the types of special talents they possess. Like you, they were all placed privately with extremely wealthy couples who wanted a child so badly they were willing to take an adolescent." She extended a sheet of paper to him and he scanned it eagerly.

"Grace, Mark, Faith...Gideon. No last names?"

She spoke again. "And those first names may not be correct anymore. A friend of your father's helped us escape after he was killed. He tried to undo some of the brainwashing that you all were subjected to but he only was partially successful. I also asked him to give you new names but he told me he only could implant new names in Grace and Mark. You apparently were too resistant and Faith got too upset."

"So what are the two new names? And what are their last names?"

"I don't know. I asked him not to tell me so that if anyone ever found me they wouldn't be able to get information about you from me."

Jake lifted his head from the piece of paper and she could see the deep shock of knowledge in his eyes as he realized how much she had given up to keep her children safe. "You're not kidding about any of this."

She shook her head. "I wish I was."

"What's the asterisk here beside Gideon's name?"

"He's the one I left behind." Saying it aloud was enough to bring tears to her eyes. The agonizing memory seared into her brain, of her young son's face as she turned and ran, caused the tears to run down her cheeks. She would never forgive herself for not saving Gideon as well. She should have died trying.

But then the others wouldn't have made it, reminded the inner voice that had kept her going each time she'd castigated herself through the years. "Gideon had a nickname. That nickname is why I'm so sure he was involved in the World Bank Heist."

Jake's expression altered, and she saw that he knew what she meant.

"Achilles," he whispered. "Jesus. My own brother."

She nodded. "It's the name you and Grace gave him when he was little." The happier thought made her smile a little. "His gifts include an extraordinary capability with technology, which gave him the means to orchestrate the robbery. Achilles was the code name used for it, the name that the police uncovered." The smile faded.

"It's awfully convenient, isn't it?" Jake's voice was thoughtful, his expression absorbed.

"What is?"

"I've wondered right from the beginning why this group gave out any information about themselves. Why they revealed Achilles as the name of the mastermind.'' His eyes narrowed. ''They wanted to find out if you're alive, didn't they? They used Gideon as a decoy, probably figuring you wouldn't be able to resist trying to save him. And if they can get you and force you to tell them what you did with the rest of us... They're trying to smoke us out, aren't they?''

Violet only nodded, her throat so choked by fear that she couldn't speak.

Jake slowly, carefully folded the piece of paper and tucked it into his wallet. He stood again and crossed the floor to her, gently setting his hands at her shoulders and turning her so that she could see their reflections in the mirror above the polished mantel. For a long moment, she simply drank in the sight of her son. Her son! Standing right behind her, a full head taller than she was now but with the same dark hair and his father's unmistakable features.

''You really are my mother, aren't you?'' His voice was just a murmur in her ear, stirring the wavy curls at her temples.

She nodded slowly, fighting tears. ''I really am your mother.''

Three

"I don't care what you did or didn't learn out in Podunk, Texas." The vicious undertone that ran beneath the smooth voice was more evident than usual.

"Going to Greenlaurel was helpful. And we're very close to finding the rest of them," said Agnes Payne in a sweetly reasonable tone. She had to work not to let the apprehension she was feeling seep into her voice.

"Close isn't good enough!" Now the voice grew strident. "We know Jake Ingram is aware of us now, thanks to your ineptitude in snatching up the wrong Ingram son. Do not, I repeat, *do not* underestimate his intellectual capabilities."

"I could hardly forget when I was one of the people who raised him." Agnes's voice held more than a touch of ice. "And I told you before, if you insist on hiring less-than-adequate help, Oliver and I can't be responsible for the consequences."

"Tell him about Grace," whispered Oliver Grimble from his seat at her side.

Agnes shook her head violently as she listened a moment more. Then she said, "We will. And we'll be in touch in a few days.'' With that, she slammed down the telephone handset so hard the bottom panel flew off and the batteries fell out.

Oliver scrambled to pick them up and put the phone back together again. ''Croft will be thrilled when we get Grace,'' he assured Agnes.

''*If* we get her,'' Agnes snapped. ''We aren't positive this Gretchen Wagner person is our Grace.''

''She has to be. She's the right age. She was adopted at the age of twelve. She had a wildly accelerated educational curve. And remember the pictures in *National Geographic?* Gretchen Wagner looks like Violet.'' He shivered. ''For so long we thought the children might be dead... What if Violet survived as well?''

''If she did, we'll find her,'' promised Agnes. ''She won't be able to resist contacting us once she realizes Gideon's alive. And then we'll deal with her the way we did with Henry.'' Her face was no longer composed, but contorted with anger. ''I want to hear something on that girl soon,'' she hissed.

''We will,'' Oliver soothed. ''But I'm telling you, it's her. Look at her accomplishments. They're exactly what we would have expected from Grace, with her talents for languages and decoding.''

''Kurt Miller had better report in soon.'' Agnes checked her watch. ''He said he thought he might make first contact today.''

Kurt escorted Gretchen from the restaurant. As the evening had drawn to a close, she had gotten desperately chatty. He could only imagine what she feared might happen next.

"Gretchen?" He reached out and touched a finger to her lips.

Above his hand, her eyes were enormous. "What?"

"Would you like me to escort you to your room?"

"M-my room? Why, no, that's all right. I'm perfectly fine. I—"

"Okay." An elevator stood open and Kurt gently nudged her inside, then punched the button for her floor before stepping back out of the car. "Then I'll see you tomorrow evening at seven in the lobby."

His eyes locked with hers until the doors slid closed and the car began to ascend. Then he turned and headed for the bar. Damn, he needed a drink. He would have escorted her to her room, probably should have, but he'd sensed a massive dose of nerves. If he'd tried to stay with her right up until she reached the door of her room she might have thought he expected to come in.

Which he didn't, although he was pretty sure that if she were a different kind of woman, more confident and cosmopolitan—and not the target of an investigation—he'd have seduced her in a New York minute. She turned him on more than any woman he'd ever met, although he wasn't really sure why.

She was slightly taller than average and nicely built, as far as he could tell beneath the rather shapeless clothing she'd worn every time he'd seen her so far. Her hair was thick and dark and her eyes were a deep, clear blue. She had a straight little nose and a full lower lip that he was dying to taste. All in all, a very attractive package, although he imagined a lot of men overlooked her appeal. Gretchen Wagner didn't invite male attention. In fact, she almost seemed to avoid it. She walked with an abstracted air as if she were thinking faraway thoughts, her head down and her eyes averted. She definitely wasn't giving off any "interested and available" signs, and he'd bet she flew right under most men's radar.

Before tonight, the times she'd seemed most alive and tuned in to her surroundings were the times he'd seen her with her assistant. Then he'd seen flashes of humor and a charmingly shy sensual awareness. Tonight, she'd blossomed beneath his interest, her pretty face glowing, her eyes blazing with intensity and a formidable intellect when she'd realized he was interested in what she had to say.

Yes, a very attractive package. But that still didn't explain the fevered interest he felt. His pulse raced and his whole body hummed when she smiled into his eyes. What would happen if she ever actually touched him? He didn't get it. No woman had ever made him feel like this before.

"Kurt? Well, I'll be damned." A hand reached out and pounded him on the back and he turned.

"Max Strong." Kurt shook his head, stunned to see a face from home. "It sure is a small world."

"It is, indeed." Max indicated the bar stool beside him. "Sit. Catch me up on the life and times of a private investigator."

Kurt shrugged. "I'm here on a job. What's your excuse?" Privately, he was a little shocked by his one-time employer's appearance. Max's clothes hung loosely on his six-foot frame and there were dark circles beneath his brown eyes despite a deep tan.

Max made a movement of dismissal with one hand. "Beats being in the States." He motioned the bartender to bring Kurt a drink. "But damn, I'm tired of jumping around."

Max had been married when Kurt had taken on a job investigating a potential real-estate deal several years ago, but according to recent news reports the marriage had gone up in smoke. Exceedingly wealthy in his own right, Max had immediately become the world's number-one available bachelor. Until now, Kurt had found it amusing, but clearly it wasn't amusing Max. There had been speculation that Strong was suffering from mental illness, although the only illness Kurt thought he appeared to have was exhaustion.

"I was sorry to hear about your father's death and your marriage ending," Kurt said carefully.

"Thank you for the first. On the second, don't be." Max tossed back the contents of the shot glass in front of him in one neat gulp. "She married me for money and she's pissed because she isn't going to get it. End of story."

"She hassling you?"

"She would if she could find me."

"What else are you running from?"

Max's lips twisted. "The press. My family. My attorney and a long parade of nervous business associates who seem to think my companies are going to go under without me." He held up a finger. "Which, by the way, is a crock. I hire exceedingly capable people and pay them a damned fortune for their loyalty and expertise."

"You sound like you need a vacation."

"That's what I thought." Max signaled for another drink. "But I might as well be at home. Reporters are in my face everywhere I turn. Right behind them are a bunch of women who don't even know me angling for the newly opened position of wife."

"The women would be all right, but I can see why the thought of another wife curdles your blood." Then a thought struck him. "I'm taking a vacation after I wrap up this job," Kurt said. "You could join me." For some reason, Gretchen's face sprang into his head. He could *not* get involved with a client, he reminded himself. Still, once the job was over, there was no law that said he couldn't see her again, was there?

"Where are you going for your R & R?" Max asked.

Kurt snorted as he raised the glass of imported German beer. "You've never heard of it."

"Try me."

"Brunhia."

Max's eyebrows rose. "Where is Brunhia? I thought my grasp of geography was above average but you've stumped me."

"Brunhia is an island off the coast of Portugal," Kurt told him. "It's only about four miles long and a mile wide with two tiny fishing villages, a lot of rocks and heavily wooded land."

Max's eyebrows shot clear up to his hairline. "And the attraction is…?"

"Nobody would have a clue where you are." Kurt grinned again. "I own a good portion of the island, several played-out marble mines and a house at the far end of the island from the villages."

"Ah." Max clearly was waiting for more information.

"I had this sort of crazy uncle," he added. "He discovered significant quantities of marble on the island in the fifties. Being the astute, environmentally sensitive guy that he was, Uncle Reg mined the hell out of the marble until there was none left. He built a house and used a boatload of the marble in it and lived there off and on until he died a couple of years ago. Being the only heir, I was the lucky recipient of the estate."

"I see."

"You can't possibly," Kurt told him dryly. "There's nothing, absolutely nothing to do unless you want to fish with the locals. It's quiet, completely isolated and damn near impossible to get to from any angle other than the cove where the villages are.'' He laughed. ''I love it when I'm in need of solitude.''

''Sounds great.'' There was a note of longing in Max's tone that surprised Kurt.

''It is. I went there for a couple of months after I left the force in Baltimore. It was…good for my soul.'' He studied Max. ''It would be good for you, too. No one would know you were there.''

''Thanks, but I'll pass. I'd feel like I was imposing.'' His friend managed a smile but Kurt sensed a resignation, a sense of having given up, that concerned him. The Maxwell Strong who'd once hired him had been assertive, entertaining and unflappable. The man sitting beside him was making an effort, but something vital was missing.

''It's a big place,'' he said. ''Six bedrooms. I'd love the company.'' He balled a fist and lightly struck Max in the upper arm. ''Come on. It's not every day you get invited to visit someplace *you've* never been.''

Max grimaced. ''You're right about that.'' But he didn't accept the invitation. ''I need to be able to access the Net, though. My employees are great with the day-to-day stuff, but I make any major decisions.'' He made a face. ''Especially since the World Bank Heist.''

''Did you take a hit?'' Kurt knew too many people who had seen their retirement investments vanish almost overnight.

"Not badly." Max shook his head. "But it's a balancing act and I can't afford to be out of touch."

"You wouldn't have to be. There's service installed."

"Well..."

"Here's what we'll do." He almost had him, Kurt was sure of it. "I'm wrapping up this job inside of a week or two. Why don't I call the caretakers and arrange for you to go right away? If I took you to the airport early tomorrow in disguise, you could get out of here unobserved. I'll join you when my job is finished."

Still Max hesitated.

Kurt decided to go for broke. "Look, buddy, you look like hell and you seem to feel even worse. You're going to Brunhia tomorrow." He reached out and shoved the full shot glass away from his friend's hand. "Go get a good night's sleep and I'll come by your room in the morning."

Max grinned, and for the first time, a glimmer of the old spirit showed through. "When you ask so nicely, how can I resist?" Then his face sobered. He stood and clasped a hand on Kurt's shoulder for a brief moment, squeezing hard. "You're a good guy, Miller. You know that?"

Gretchen answered the knock on the door of her hotel room the following evening with a smile, unable to hide the pleasure and anticipation she was feeling at the thought of another evening with Kurt

Miller. But she'd thought they'd agreed to meet in the lobby. Her palms instantly grew clammy. She wasn't prepared yet to see him again.

When the door swung open to reveal her assistant, it was a toss-up as to who was more surprised.

"Hey, Dr. Wagner!" Nancy's eyes shone. "You look really hot. I didn't even know you owned stuff like that."

"Thanks, I think." Gretchen felt heat climb her cheeks. "I bought it in one of the boutiques downstairs after we got back today."

"So what's the occasion? I came by to talk you into coming along with us tonight, but—" Nancy waved a hand vaguely in the air "—it looks like you've already got plans."

"I have a date." She felt weird even saying the word aloud. Gretchen Wagner didn't date.

Nancy's mouth fell open. "Well, you sly fox, you! And here I was worrying about you getting out of your room once in a while."

Gretchen was warmed by the younger woman's thoughtfulness. She smiled. "I appreciate the thought, though." Then apprehension took over again. "Do I look all right?" She smoothed a hand down over the slim black cocktail dress she'd bought. "I bought the shoes, too," she confessed.

"You look terrific," Nancy said sincerely. "Understated elegance with a hint of sex appeal."

"Only a hint?" Gretchen pouted. Then she

clapped a hand over her mouth. "That was *not* me talking."

"Whatever you say. But just for the record, men *love* a hint of sex appeal. Most men like it a lot more than having a shelf of half-naked boobs shoved in their face."

Gretchen's eyes widened. "Who would do that?"

Nancy shook her head. "Doc, you are just too naive to be believed. Do you walk around with blinders on?"

"Well, actually, I'm usually so engrossed in my thoughts that I'm not very observant when it comes to people."

"I'm headed downstairs," Nancy said. "If you're almost ready, I'll wait."

"Just let me get my purse," Gretchen said. She grimaced. "Why in the world anyone wants to carry a purse when they could just as easily toss a backpack over a shoulder is beyond me."

The two women headed downstairs. As the elevator doors opened onto the lobby level, the first thing Gretchen saw was Kurt Miller lounging against a glass-and-brass railing around a display of plants.

He straightened, his brown eyes warm on her face, then leisurely sliding down over her figure in the black dress. Gretchen felt an irrational urge to hide.

"I can feel the heat from here," Nancy murmured sotto voce.

Gretchen didn't answer. Kurt had started across the

floor. Her mouth was dry, her feet felt rooted to the spot.

"I'll just get going now. You have a great evening." Nancy's tone was amused as she moved away from the elevators toward the lobby doors.

"Hello." Kurt's voice was deep and husky. "You look lovely tonight."

"So do you," she blurted. Then, as his eyes crinkled, she added, "Look very nice, I mean."

"I know what you meant." He offered her an arm, and when she slipped her fingers through the crook of his elbow, he covered her small hand with his own much larger, much rougher one. Her palm was pressed against the casual navy blazer he wore with a pair of charcoal pants, but she could feel corded muscle beneath. He steered her toward the most elegant of the restaurants in the hotel. "Do you like French cuisine?"

"I'll eat just about anything," she told him. "Is that what they serve here?"

He nodded. His head was bent down toward her, making her feel small and feminine. "And there's a Viennese orchestra."

"It sounds lovely."

"It is." He was looking at her face and she had the distinct impression that he hadn't meant the orchestra.

Flustered, she looked away.

Above her head she heard him chuckle. Then he spoke to the maître d', who led them to their table.

But Kurt didn't let her sit down. Instead, he held out a hand. "Shall we dance?"

"Oh," she said, "I don't dance. But thank you."

But he took her hand in his. "Why don't you dance? Don't you like to?"

"I don't know. I never learned."

"Then here's your chance."

"No! Kurt, wait!" But it was like trying to stop a tank. "I hope you can dance better than I can or we're in trouble," she muttered as he tugged her toward the dance floor.

He must have overheard her, because as he turned and held out his arms, he said, "I can dance. I'll have you know I've attended my share of balls."

"Balls? Good grief, I thought those had gone out with the Civil War." She let him put her right hand in his and her left on his shoulder. Then, as he slid his left arm around her waist, she took a deep, nervous breath.

"Not in Texas," he said wryly.

She chuckled. "What are they like?"

"Nothing special. You know," he said vaguely.

"No," she said, "I don't know. We don't do things like that in the Northeast very much and certainly not in the academics circles in which I move."

He shrugged. "Men have to wear monkey suits." He grinned. "Women call them tuxes. All the ladies get dressed to the nines in long gowns and every diamond they own. Everyone pretends to be polite and friendly, there's dancing and drinking and usually some kind of interesting scene or two before the night is over."

Gretchen laughed aloud. "Sounds like fun."

"Spoken like a woman," he said dryly.

"Well, what do you expect?" she asked. "I *am* a woman."

Kurt looked down at her, and there was no humor lurking in his eyes now. "Believe me, I'm aware of that fact."

She suddenly realized they were moving around the dance floor, their bodies close. Kurt was so smooth and easy to follow she hadn't even realized how fluidly they were dancing together. Immediately her body tensed. Her hand tightened in his and she clutched at his shoulder as she stumbled.

"Whoa, there, Professor. Relax."

"I can't dance," she said. "Let's sit down."

But Kurt ignored the suggestion. "You were doing fine until you thought about it," he said. "Just pretend you're at a ball."

"I've never even been to a high school dance," she said. "So I'm thinking that's not going to happen."

He laughed aloud. Then, seeing that she was serious, he asked, "Why didn't you ever go to a dance? I refuse to believe that no guy ever noticed how pretty you are."

The compliment thrilled her, even though she knew she wasn't someone men looked at twice. "I finished high school at age fifteen." It wasn't a boast but an explanation. ''My childhood was...unique and I never really had the chance or the inclination to develop relationships with other people my own age.''

''Why not?'' Then he grimaced. ''If you graduated at fifteen, you must have been seriously academically accelerated.''

''I was.'' She took a breath. ''I was too different to have much in common with my same-age peers, and yet I was too young to have anything in common with those in my classes. That only got worse when I started college at sixteen.''

He nodded. ''I can see how that would be a problem. Kids can be rough on anyone who's different.''

''I was very lucky to have wonderful parents. They were told when I was adopted that I had special academic needs, and they devoted themselves to helping me.''

''Wait a minute. How could they know you were so smart? Babies are babies.''

''But I was twelve years old when I was adopted,'' she said.

She sensed his shock. ''*Twelve?* What happened to your biological family? If you don't mind talking about it,'' he added hastily.

She shrugged. ''There's really nothing to talk about. I don't know anything about my birth parents.''

''So you grew up in an orphanage? Why weren't you adopted earlier?''

"No." He was clearly confused and she couldn't blame him. "I think I was raised by my birth parents for at least part of that time, but I don't have any memory of it."

"You don't have any memory of it." He was silent for a moment. Then he shook his head. "Tell me more. But first, let's get back to our table and order."

A few minutes later, the waiter departed and Kurt looked at her expectantly. "No memory...?" he prompted. Why hadn't Oliver Gamble warned him? Maybe he didn't know. Apparently, the man had been separated from his daughter years ago.

"Nothing significant," she said. "A few tiny things, impressions really, but that's it."

"I can't imagine that. Is there any reason that they know of for you to have lost your memory?"

She shook her head. "My parents took me to a psychologist at our family doctor's recommendation. All they could tell me was that there is no physiological reason for my amnesia." She grimaced. "Apparently I just have a selective mind."

"Isn't memory loss often associated with trauma?" he asked.

"Yes, but I was perfectly healthy when I was adopted. No signs of trauma." She rested her chin on one hand and her face was pensive.

"Unbelievable." Kurt picked up his drink and his expression was wry when he said, "What I wouldn't give for a little amnesia and you're stuck with it."

She looked at him quizzically. "You'd *like* to lose your memory?"

"Of some things." *Like being accused of the murder of your partner on the job. Like being dumped by your fiancée for being too honest.* Yeah, there were a few things he wouldn't mind wiping out of his memory banks. But all he said was, "I'm sure everybody has at least one event in their life they'd like to forget."

"I've got one." Gretchen was smiling, a relaxed, spontaneous expression that he hadn't seen before. He wondered if it was the excellent French wine they were drinking, his company or simply that it took her this long to relax and unwind at the end of the day.

"Okay. Try me."

"A couple of years ago I was giving a lecture in Chicago and I graciously thanked the people of Minneapolis for having me there."

Kurt chuckled.

"I was in Minneapolis the day before that," she said plaintively.

"Mine's better," he said. "When I was a young cop on the beat—"

"You were a police officer?"

"Yeah, before I decided to go to work for myself." And this wasn't a topic he wanted to get started on tonight. "Anyway, I was standing there taking a witness's statement one day when the guy's dog mistook me for a fire hydrant."

"Mine was more public," she said.

"The dog was a Great Dane."

"Oh." After a moment she started to grin, then to giggle. She pursed her lips and stopped, but then her laughing eyes met his and she burst into gales of laughter that brought tears to her eyes. She dabbed at them with her napkin, and when she finally had calmed down enough to speak, she said, "Sorry. I just had this vivid mental picture of you." She broke up again.

"Just for that," he said, "you owe me another dance after dinner."

"No problem."

"And this time we're doing the tango."

Her eyebrows rose. "Why do I fear that might precipitate another of those moments neither of us would like to remember?"

"I can't imagine ever wanting to forget a single moment with you." The words had come out without thought, and as soon as he uttered them he was sorry. It was only their second date and that had sounded far too serious. *Way to go, Miller. Way to chase away the prettiest lady you've ever been lucky enough to go out with.*

But Gretchen didn't look scared. She looked... shocked. Her beautiful blue eyes searched his face as if she were waiting for him to retract the words.

The moment stretched between them, but still she didn't speak.

"Gretchen?" He reached across the table and laid

his hand over one of hers. "I'm sorry if I spoke out of turn. I didn't mean to make you feel uncomfortable."

"You didn't," she said, almost as if the fact surprised her. "I was just… No one's ever said anything that lovely to me before," she finished with painful honesty.

Kurt felt his heart contract. Dammit. Gretchen Wagner was a job. He couldn't get involved with her. And yet, he knew beyond a doubt that walking away was no longer an option. She was too damned innocent, too naive and unaware of her own charm to be running around on her own.

Somebody had to take care of her.

Four

After their meals, they danced again. Not the tango, as he'd threatened, but a couple of sweet, slow tunes on the low-lit dance floor, in an intimate cocoon of their own making in the midst of a press of other couples.

The dance floor grew very crowded. Only in a European hotel such as theirs was such close contact between men and women permissible. The conservative, Islamic societies of most Middle Eastern countries meant entertainment options could be a little limited. As the evening wore on, Kurt held her closer, then closer still, drawing her in until their bodies brushed lightly and his lips were within a mere breath of her temple.

Gretchen had never known such utterly sweet feelings before. In her entire life she'd only had one relationship of any kind. That experience had been with a professor many years her senior and had been less than romantic from start to finish, leaving her to wonder why people made such a fuss over love. All she'd been left with were feelings of discomfort, outright embarrassment and humiliation that she'd been so stupid.

Tonight, for the very first time, she thought she might understand. In Kurt's arms she felt beautiful and desirable. His eyes were warm and admiring, his embrace both protective and excitingly possessive. She thought she might be happy simply to dance like this for the rest of her life.

Then the band took a break.

"Rats," she said as the bandleader announced they'd be back in just a little while. "I don't want to stop dancing."

Kurt grinned. "Good. That's exactly what I was thinking."

He put a hand at her back and guided her to their table, where they ordered something to drink. She noted that like her, Kurt was getting something non-alcoholic and she was secretly pleased. She'd never been much of a drinker. The wine they'd had with dinner was almost more than her limit and she wouldn't have felt comfortable with a man who drank a lot.

Then Kurt reached across the table and covered her hand with his. "Thank you for having dinner with me tonight. When I found out I had to come to Egypt, I didn't expect to enjoy it quite so much."

"Why did you have to come to Egypt?" She deliberately phrased it the same way he just had.

His expression changed, becoming unreadable, and she immediately realized what she'd said. "Oh, I'm sorry. I forgot you probably can't talk about your work."

"No." He shook his head and his shoulders visibly relaxed. "I can't, except in the most general terms."

"How long have you been a private investigator?"

"About eight years."

"And how did you get into this kind of work?" She smiled. "University professors are a dime a dozen but I can't say I've ever met a private eye before."

He looked amused. "I, on the other hand, have met a lot more of the latter than of the former." He picked up his drink and took a gulp.

Gretchen nodded, studying him thoughtfully. "You said you started out as a policeman. I can imagine you as a cop. What made you choose that career?"

"I was always interested in law enforcement," he said. "Our next-door neighbor was a cop when I was growing up and I thought he was the greatest guy in the world." He smiled, but the expression was bittersweet. "I used to pretend he was my father. Of course, I wanted to be a cop, too."

Her heart was touched. She could imagine the little boy who'd lost his own parents wishing that he still fit into a traditional family, even though his grandmother clearly had given him plenty of love and encouragement. But she sensed he wouldn't welcome an amateur psychoanalyst. "So what made you move into this work?"

A muscle jumped in his jaw and the warmth drained from his face. "Being a cop wasn't the honorable profession I'd expected it to be. I'd rather work for myself."

She didn't know what to say in response. "It wasn't honorable?"

"No." His brown eyes met hers, but he didn't elaborate.

In the single word, though, she heard disillusionment, sadness, resignation—a host of unhappy overtones. "Tell me what happened," she said softly.

He shrugged as if it was no big deal, but she sensed there was a lot more to the story. "There was a lot of corruption in my department. Either you played along or you got targeted for trouble."

"What kind of trouble?"

He hesitated for a moment, and she thought he wasn't going to say anything more.

She raised her eyebrows and cocked her head expectantly.

"During a drug raid, my partner was shot in the back." His voice was flat. "I was accused of killing him until Ballistics matched the bullets to another gun."

It was hard to credit what he seemed to be telling her. "Your fellow officers set you up?"

His lips twisted. "They wanted me off the force any way they could manage it," he said. "If I hadn't found cover, they'd have shot me, too, and then put the gun that had killed Rayford, my partner, in my hand.''

''Why would they do that?''

''I found out that a group of my fine fellow officers had a side business as independent narcotics dealers. They were confiscating crack and then reselling most of each bust. They thought I was going to turn them in.''

''Were you?''

He managed a small smile. ''Oh, yeah.''

''You should have!'' She was horrified. ''But surely everyone in your department wasn't crooked,'' she said.

''No.'' He shrugged again. ''But when you're a career officer with retirement in sight and a family to raise, you can't afford to rock the boat.''

''You mean they wouldn't stand up for you?'' Initial outrage became anger and she didn't try to hide it.

He nodded, smiling slightly. ''Right.''

''Well, that stinks!''

His smile widened and she saw the shadows in his eyes fade. ''Yeah, it does. But hey, look where I am now. I like this job a whole lot better than I ever liked being a cop.'' He reached across the table and took her hand, his thumb lightly stroking across her knuckles. ''Especially right now.''

She wanted to talk more about his experience with the police force, but she sensed he wasn't comfortable with the topic and she was enjoying the evening too much to pursue something that might mar it. Besides, his heavy-lidded eyes were warm and interested, and his hand was sending small streamers of heat flowing through her.

Kurt Miller was walking sex appeal, and she suspected he knew it. If she were smart, she'd run to her room and not come out until it was time to go back to Boston.

But the band came back then and struck up a slow, romantic tune and she couldn't resist when he tugged her to her feet and headed for the dance floor again.

This time he made little attempt to preserve a distance between them, drawing her close so that she could feel the heat of his hard body all along the length of hers. It was erotic, arousing, enticing, and she had to resist the unfamiliar urge to rub her body against his, to press her aching breasts against his broad chest and brush her hips against him, to learn the angles and contours of his hard body.

Above her head, his breathing increased. "Ah, baby," he growled, "you're going to kill me."

Her? Gretchen Wagner, who'd never been to a prom, never been asked to dance a single time in her life? It was unreal, and accordingly, she decided to enjoy it. For as long as it lasted.

She laid her head on his shoulder and let him guide her to the lazy beat of the music through the rest of the set, giving herself this man and this moment so that when she was back in her lonely little world at home she could pull out the memory. Then she could remind herself that at least once in her life she'd been found attractive, desirable, interesting. None of which she was for real.

The thought deflated a little of her pleasure in the evening. As if he sensed the change in her mood, Kurt said, "You're not happy. What's wrong?"

She shook her head slightly, not lifting it from his shoulder, and her mouth brushed the pulse in his neck where his dress shirt was opened at the throat. "Nothing," she whispered.

She felt a shudder run through him. He lowered his head and when he spoke again, his mouth was against her cheek. "Professor." His voice was rough and low, rumbling up from the depths of his chest and he made the word sound like an endearment.

She lifted her head the slightest bit. "Hmm?"

In answer, he angled his head and slid his mouth over hers.

Gretchen responded instantly, too overwhelmed by the unfamiliar feelings rushing through her to even consider denying him. She shuddered when his tongue traced the line of her lips, and when he exerted the smallest pressure, she opened her mouth slowly in response, allowing his tongue to sweep in and search out all the sweet places inside.

The sensation turned her insides to liquid, and she felt an insistent throbbing deep between her thighs. Recklessly, she pressed herself closer to him, sandwiching the tantalizing ridge of his shockingly hard flesh between them, making him groan. "Baby, you're killing me," he panted against her mouth.

He kissed her hard and deep several more times until she wouldn't even have thought of saying no to anything he wanted.

But when she was hanging helplessly in his arms, Kurt finally gentled the kisses, nuzzling along the line of her jaw as her head lolled back against his hard arm.

"Dammit," he said between his teeth. "I'm sorry, Professor."

She was bewildered. What would he be sorry for? A little of the hot glow of pleasure dimmed and she was suddenly ashamed of her abandoned behavior. A deep blush crawled up her neck and she ducked her head as she attempted to pull free from his encircling arms.

But Kurt wouldn't let her go. He quelled her efforts to pull herself free. "Where are you going?"

She made her body stiff. "To bed." She tried for nonchalance, but there was a quiver in her voice that she couldn't suppress. "I have a lot of work to do tomorrow."

"You're upset," he said. "What can I say to make this better?"

She was silent, head down. She was terrible at any kind of confrontation, courtesy of her total lack of experience.

There was a brief hesitation before he said, "I'm

sorry if I came on too strong. I suppose saying you overwhelmed my common sense is a poor excuse."

Her brow knitted and she looked up at him finally. "I did what?"

"Overwhelmed my common sense." He sounded almost embarrassed. "I'm not the kind of guy who goes around pawing women on a regular basis."

"I didn't mind," she said in a small voice.

"You—" He stopped. "You're not mad at me for taking advantage of you?"

"You didn't take advantage of me."

Kurt stared down at her for a long minute. "Gretchen," he said at last, "exactly why are you mad at me?"

"I wouldn't characterize myself as 'mad,'" she informed him. "Piqued might be a better word."

He rolled his eyes. "All right. Why are you *piqued* at me?" He gave the word an inflection that suggested it was in quotation marks.

"You stopped," she said before she could let herself think about the wisdom of engaging in this kind of provocative conversation.

"Stopped?" He looked lost. He shook his head, apparently not following.

"You stopped kissing me," she said concisely, each word carefully enunciated, "and then you said you were sorry. I assumed you were sorry for kissing me."

"I was." Again he stopped her before she could break free. "Not sorry that I kissed you to start with,'' he specified. ''Only sorry that we have to stop.''

''I wasn't going to stop you,'' she said.

''I know!'' It was almost a roar and he immediately lowered his voice as couples around them turned to look at them. ''And I damn near didn't, either. Don't you get it?'' He shook his head, a wry grin beginning to curl at the corners of his mouth. ''When you step away from me, it's going to be very evident to anyone watching that you turn me on in a big way. If we don't stop here, we're going to finish it in your room or mine, and I don't think you're ready for that.''

She was so shocked she didn't know what to say. ''Oh.''

His response was a hissed curse as he shook his head. ''Dammit, woman. You're dangerous.''

Taking her by the shoulders, he turned her around and kept her in front of him as they returned to their table. He sat immediately but kept her standing by his side. ''Listen,'' he said. ''You're leaving now. Go straight to your room and go to bed.''

''What are you going to do?''

His grin was lopsided, his eyes laughing. ''I'm not going anywhere for a few minutes until I'm a little less…''

''Obvious?'' she suggested with a spurt of daring she hadn't had at the beginning of the evening.

''I wouldn't have been so polite, but yeah, that works.'' He slipped an arm around her waist and drew her close, sliding one hand up to pull her head down to his. He kissed her deep and hard, stealing her breath and throwing her body into turmoil before setting her away from him. "Go. Now. I'll call you tomorrow and we'll have dinner again."

"All right." In a daze, she turned and walked away. But when she got to the entrance of the restaurant, she looked over her shoulder. Kurt was watching her with naked hunger. He wore an unfamiliar, utterly male expression that made her insides shiver in response. Hesitantly, she lifted a hand and wiggled her fingers at him.

His expression didn't change, but he slowly lifted a hand in return.

Warmth spread through her, and she sent him a brilliant smile before heading in the direction of the elevators.

Halfway to her room, she recalled his last words and was briefly miffed that he'd simply assumed she would be free for dinner. But the annoyance couldn't last as she relived the events of the evening.

Kurt Miller was interested in her. Genuinely attracted. To her! She should pinch herself, but she was enjoying herself too much to chance reality.

He couldn't feel worse about it if he tried, Kurt decided over breakfast. Well, that wasn't true. If he'd seduced Gretchen, he'd feel worse.

But that was little comfort. Neither was telling himself he'd never behaved so unprofessionally before, that she'd bypassed every ounce of common sense he'd ever possessed and made him want her so badly he'd completely forgotten that she was just a job.

Gretchen would never be "just" anything.

That thought brought him up short. *You have no business getting involved with her, he reminded himself. And once you put her in contact with her father, you'll never see her again.*

It didn't set well. But neither did his own actions, which brought him back to the truth of the matter again.

He'd taken terrible advantage of a mutual attraction to pump Gretchen Wagner for information—information that only solidified his belief that she was the woman he'd been hired to find.

Checking his watch, he saw that it was early afternoon back on the East Coast, time to check in with his employer. He should have done so sooner, but he really hadn't had anything to report until now.

Finishing his solitary meal, he paid his tab and returned to his room, where he put through a call to the States.

"Hello?"

"Mr. Gamble?" *Gretchen Gamble. Had that been her name?* "This is Kurt Miller."

"Miller!" The voice was strident, relief and irritation warring in the overly loud tone. "Where are you? Why haven't you called?"

"I didn't have anything to report," said Kurt evenly. "I—"

"We— I expect to be kept apprised of every day's events, even if you feel there is nothing to report." Gamble paused. "So what do you have for us? For me?"

"I observed Gretchen Wagner and then made contact. Subsequent conversations have revealed some of the information you were seeking."

"She was adopted as an older child?"

"At the age of twelve."

"And she is an academic prodigy?"

"Most definitely." Kurt thought of the lonely teen years Gretchen had described to him.

"I'm sure it's her!" The man sounded jubilant. "All right. Here's what I need you to do now. I want you to explain to her that you represent me, that I want to meet her."

"But...she believes her biological parents are dead," Kurt said. "I can't just—"

"Of course you can." Gamble paused. "Tell her that her mother is dead and when I learned of her existence recently I've been frantic to find her ever since."

Sitting on the edge of his bed, Kurt raised a sardonic eyebrow. Gamble sounded ridiculously melodramatic. "I'll explain it," he said noncommittally.

"Arrange to bring her back to the States," Gamble instructed him. "We'll meet in three days—"

"Whoa! She's not going to agree to leave Egypt right away. She's in the middle of a job."

"But surely when you tell her that her father's alive and wants to meet her..."

Kurt allowed the silence to hang.

"I have a fortune at my disposal," Gamble said. "The girl is my heir. Don't you think that will change her priorities?"

"I can't speak for her." But God, he hoped not.

"Well, try it. Get back to me with her answer as soon as you can."

"There's something you need to know," Kurt told him. "Gretchen has no memory of her life before she was adopted."

There was a significant silence. "None?" Gamble sounded shocked but the word had an odd quality to it, almost as if he'd rehearsed it.

"She said she has a few impressions, but nothing concrete. She doesn't remember you or her mother, or anything about her life with you." He paused. "I presume you *did* have a personal relationship with her when she was a child?"

"Of course I did," Gamble snapped.

"All right. I just wanted to be sure you weren't a total stranger to your daughter."

"If she has no memory of me, I may as well be," Gamble said in a thoughtful tone. Then his voice grew brisk. "Her memory loss is irrelevant. I still want you to carry on."

After a few more curt instructions, Gamble concluded the call.

Kurt simply sat on the edge of his bed, staring at the telephone. Something in the way Gamble issued orders set his teeth on edge. At least, he hoped that was all it was. He'd never had this feeling on a case before. It was similar to the feeling he'd occasionally had as a cop when a situation that appeared to be well under control suddenly went wild.

Jake Ingram sat in the departure lounge at Dulles Airport, waiting for his flight back to Texas to be announced. It was delayed, as usual, and he was mildly annoyed with himself because he'd left *The Washington Post* he'd been reading behind in his hotel room.

He almost turned to his bodyguard but then he realized that Robert wouldn't have reading material with him; the man's job was to observe their surroundings.

He could go get a novel or another paper, but he didn't really want to leave the area. Three seats down from him, a *National Geographic* lay on an empty seat. Jake caught the eye of the woman in the seat just beyond it.

"Is that your magazine, ma'am?"

The woman smiled and shook her head. "It was here when I sat down." She picked it up and passed it down to him. "Finders keepers."

Jake returned the smile. "If someone comes hunting for it, I'll be right here until my flight is called."

Twenty minutes later his flight was called. Shortly afterward, he was seated in first class, still reading the abandoned magazine as the plane took off. He finished an article about the demise of endangered honey bees in the U.S. and turned the page to the next. It was a story full of glossy photos about a Harvard professor who was working on decrypting a set of stone tablets that represented a whole new written language thought to be older than anything yet discovered. As he read, something about the article nagged at him. In her thirties...languages...Harvard professor... A chill ran icy fingers down his spine, and he sat up straighter in his seat, leafing through the article with fingers suddenly clumsy and slow.

Violet—his biological mother, he thought, unable to completely convince himself that he'd actually found his family—had told him that his twin sister had been a whiz with languages and anything linguistically challenging. This woman, Gretchen Wagner, was the right age, and she appeared to have the right talents, or abilities, whatever one wanted to call them. The article mentioned that she was familiar with almost a dozen languages and that her specialty was untangling complex linguistic patterns.

And her name... His sister's name had been Grace, but Violet had warned him that her name had been changed. Could this Gretchen be Grace?

Was he reaching for straws just because of the new

information he'd received? Seeing links where only coincidences existed? He was breathing hard as he flipped through the pages trying to find a good likeness of the Harvard educator. There were several shots of Gretchen Wagner, Ph.D., with her head down or her face largely hidden as she bent over to fit pieces of the broken tablets together or cleaned the carved symbols with a delicate little brush. She had dark hair, but that was hardly conclusive identification. And then he turned to the final page of the article.

There, in full, stunning color, was a straight-on photograph of a smiling Professor Wagner. She was taller than average and slender, her hair dark and wavy, her eyes as blue as his.

But more shocking, she was a living, breathing, younger version of the woman he'd just left behind in Washington, D.C.

The resemblance took his breath away and he closed the magazine as his brain scrambled to assimilate the new reality. He had found his sister Grace. Any doubt that Violet Hobson had been telling him the truth vanished as his mind raced.

If he had found her so easily, it was more than likely that Willard Croft and the others Violet had described could find her as well. Someone as high profile as Gretchen Wagner, with a specialized field of study in which there could be few others so proficient, was an easy target for the coalition of which Violet had warned him.

He decided that he had to call Harvard University and locate Gretchen Wagner.

And then he had to make arrangements to visit her and convince her that the incredible story he had to share with her was true.

Five

"Hello?" The nasal masculine voice was impatient and rushed.

"It's Agnes."

"Do you have something?" The tone betrayed the importance of the answer.

"We found Grace." Agnes Payne shifted her grip on the telephone.

"You found her!" Croft was jubilant. "How soon can you get her and bring her to me?"

"We're working on that," Agnes said cautiously. "She's high profile. We hope to convince her to come on her own rather than having to…use force."

"Where is she?"

"Egypt."

"Egypt? Doing what?"

"She's an ancient language specialist. She's translating something. Pick up a copy of this month's *National Geographic.* There's an article about her, and when you see her, you'll know right away how we recognized her."

"I repeat—" Croft's voice grew soft and somehow more dangerous "—when can you bring her to me?"

Me, thought Agnes angrily. As if she and Oliver weren't as deeply invested in this as Croft. "I don't know. We hired a private investigator who's reporting to us. I'll keep you informed." And with that, she stabbed the off button with a vicious finger.

When she returned from work that day, Gretchen had a message waiting. When she called the desk, they sent someone right up with a delivery for her. A delivery? She tried and failed to recall any texts or materials she'd ordered recently. Maybe it wasn't really hers.

But when she opened the door to the bellboy's knock, she was shocked to see him half-obscured behind a vase of large and fragrant flowers. The card very clearly was addressed to her, and she sent the man away with a generous tip before she pounced on the little white message. She'd only received flowers once before, from her parents on her high school graduation. The card read: *Professor—Sorry I stopped. K.M.*

She laughed aloud in sheer delight, shaking her head as she replaced the card. The man was incorrigible and if she had any sense at all, she'd run the other way.

But she had no intention of running anywhere. Kurt was the most fascinating, appealing man she'd ever known. She could hardly believe he was interested in her!

Since it was already well after five and he'd asked her to meet him at six, she took the world's fastest shower, brushed out her shoulder-length dark hair and twisted it into a careless knot, and donned one of the long, loose dresses she favored in the Egyptian climate. At the last moment she took one of the lovely lilies from the fragrant bouquet and tucked it into her hair just above her left ear.

He was waiting for her in the lobby, and she actually felt the breath leave her lungs in a *whoosh* when his warm brown eyes met hers. Her whole body came tinglingly alive, and she suddenly was aware of the way the dress whispered around her body, the brush of her thighs as she moved, the cool air inside the hotel that caressed her. It was sheer sexual attraction at its most compelling, she decided, because she'd certainly never felt anything like it before.

Kurt had been leaning against a pillar waiting for her. He straightened, a smile tugging at the corners of his hard mouth. "You look beautiful tonight," he told her as he reached her side. His voice was low, his gaze sincere, and she felt herself blushing.

"Thank you." She lifted her hand and let it hover near her ear. "And thank you for the flowers."

He reached out and captured her hand in his, and her whole body jolted at the simple feel of flesh on flesh. "You're welcome."

"No man has ever sent me flowers before," she confessed.

He looked down at her. "I'm glad I was the first. I'd like to share a lot of firsts with you." A funny look crossed his face, and he shook his head.

"What?"

He laughed, and there was a frustrated edge to the sound. "I didn't mean to say that."

She didn't reply. She couldn't help being a little hurt; the words had thrilled her. To have him say he hadn't really meant them was disappointing.

He made another sound of frustration. "God, how many ways can I find to stick my foot in my mouth around you?" Guiding her to an out-of-the-way corner of the lobby, he put a finger beneath her chin and lifted her face. "What I meant was that there are things we need to discuss before I tell you I've never met a woman I like as much as I like you before. But what the hell, I've already screwed up the order, so I might as well finish this. I want to see you when we get back to the States, Gretchen. In fact, I want to see a lot of you." He drew her close, his breath feathering over her ear and making her shudder. "I'm attracted to you. Not just your body, but your mind, your honesty, your sense of humor. The way you lick your lip and hesitate before you speak drives me insane. When we danced last night...well, I'm hoping you recognized how special it was, too."

She was stunned. And thrilled anew. This exciting,

compelling man was telling her things she'd never expected she would hear—and he was serious!

He stopped and took a breath, his massive chest swelling against her. "Say something."

This had to be happening to another woman. Gorgeous men like Kurt Miller didn't find bookish scholars like her wildly exciting. "Something," she managed.

He snorted. "I can see I've bowled you over with my finesse."

She could barely think, much less speak coherently, but in his wryly amused tones she heard a note of hesitant self-deprecation that rang a too-familiar chord with her. She often felt as if she'd made some social blunder that she couldn't quite identify. She quickly lifted her hands and placed them on either side of his face, enjoying the rough sensation of his whiskered jaw beneath her palms though it was obvious he'd recently shaved.

"You certainly have," she said. "But are you sure you have the right woman? I'm not exactly the type men drool over, in case you hadn't noticed."

"I hadn't noticed," he said promptly. "You're the type *this* man drools over."

She couldn't hide the smile that felt as if it lit her entire face. "I feel the same way," she said shyly. "I'd like to see you after I get back, too."

"Good. I was afraid it was just me." Kurt wrapped his arms around her and hugged her, then he moved her toward the same restaurant where they'd eaten the night before. ''I have a fondness for this place,'' he said as they followed the maître d' to their table.

They had dinner and another bottle of wine that went down so smoothly she was a little shocked when she saw the bottle was empty. Kurt told her about some of the more ridiculous moments in his investigative career and she, at his prodding, explained the Ahk Tablets project to him more fully. He asked intelligent, insightful questions that made her feel he was truly interested in her work, dry though it often sounded to the layman.

An orchestra replaced the piano that had provided dinner music and as the strains of a lovely piece filled the air, Kurt stood and held out his hand. She took it, feeling as if she were a princess in a fairy tale. It still was hard to fathom his interest in her. Kurt was handsome, what people had once called ''strapping'' with shoulders that seemed to fill doorways, and his dark eyes gleamed with good humor and intelligence. She'd seen women sizing him up over dinner and she'd been stupidly pleased that he seemed oblivious, intent only on her.

At the edge of the dance floor he turned and drew her into his arms with a smile. ''I've been waiting for this all evening,'' he said.

''So have I.'' She closed her eyes and wrapped her arms around his neck, letting him pull her close. They swayed in silence for a while and she thought she'd never felt so content, so complete, in her entire life. At least the part she remembered, she amended.

"I have a confession to make," Kurt said into her ear. She shivered, feeling her body respond to the whisper of his breath over her sensitive skin.

"Oh?" She inclined her face up to his.

His chest rose and fell as he took a deep breath, and the firm warmth of his body pressed to hers was such a heady delight she could barely concentrate on his words. "I already knew who you were when I came over to your table the other night."

"You did?" That was all? She started to settle herself more snugly against him, still adrift in the dream quality of the evening. She wasn't plain old dry Dr. Wagner anymore. Kurt Miller was attracted to her.

"Yes." His chest rose and fell again. "I was hired by your father to find you."

The words made no sense. "My father's dead," she said. She stopped dancing and leaned back so that she could see his face.

"Your biological father." Was that *pity* in his eyes?

"My..." Words failed her. The bright, shining evening dulled and tarnished even as she spoke. "Is this a joke?"

"No. Your biological father is my client." He was watching her very carefully, and she suddenly had the awful realization that he'd been watching her in much the same way every time they'd been together—not because he was interested in her, but because he'd been hired to do so. "Your biological father is quite wealthy, and you apparently are his only heir.''

''And this matters to me because...?'' She pushed against his chest, realizing how closely he still held her, and he released her immediately. ''I'm not in the least interested in your client's money.''

''It isn't just the money.'' He heard a trace of desperation creeping into his tone and he took a deep breath. ''He's your father, Gretchen, and he hopes that you might allow him to be a part of your life.''

She crossed her arms defensively. ''My father is dead. This person, if he's even for real, is merely the man who contributed the biological material that created me.''

''And you aren't in the least curious about him? How about your birth mother? He could tell you about her, I imagine.''

''How did he find me?'' The question was abrupt and demanding but she didn't care. His words jarred her, churned inside where she'd repressed the small part of her that always had wondered about these people.

''You were in a *National Geographic* article.'' Kurt spread his hands. ''He traced you to Harvard. He hired me to make first contact.''

''Which you did. Don't you think you took him a bit literally?'' Hurt gave her tongue a sharp edge.

A dull red color climbed up his cheeks as the barb struck. ''Gretchen, listen to me—''

''So you can feed me more lies?'' Inside, she was

falling apart, but she couldn't let him know. Over the years she'd had plenty of practice ignoring the cruelties of other people who didn't understand her academic prowess; she employed that practice now to calm herself, to keep her voice even and clear, hiding any hint of her true feelings. "Why didn't you tell me right away?"

"I had to be sure you were the right woman first. My employer wasn't absolutely sure you were his daughter until after I'd observed and spoken with you."

"And last night?"

He hesitated.

"You could have told me last night," she said, trying desperately to hide the devastation she felt. "Or first thing this evening. Why did you wait?"

"Because," he said, "I was afraid you were going to react exactly like this and I wanted to hold you in my arms one more time before you kicked my teeth out."

"Consider yourself toothless," she said. Fury and a deep, searing pain colored her tone despite her best efforts. She wasn't sure who she was angrier with, him for deceiving her, or herself for being suckered into believing he might actually have found her desirable. Turning, she walked from the dance floor and the restaurant.

"Gretchen!" Kurt had to sign for the tab and she quickly made her way to the bank of elevators, ignoring the husky timbre of his voice. Thankfully, there was a car waiting at the lobby level with its doors open and she strode right in, punching the button for her floor with more force than necessary.

As she rode the elevator to her floor, she was fully aware that this was a temporary reprieve. In the past few days, as she'd grown to know Kurt, one of the things most evident about him was his strength of will. He wouldn't give up so easily.

Tears fell, hot and burning, but she brushed them away and bit her lip to still its trembling. She might have been a fool, but Kurt was a deceptive liar and she never wanted to see him again. Her agile mind flipped through his likely actions, and by the time she'd unlocked her door, she knew what she would have to do.

When she entered her room, she made a beeline for the telephone. "Yes," she said to the person at the desk who picked up. "This is Gretchen Wagner in Room two-three-two-seven. I'll be checking out immediately and I'd like you to prepare my bill."

Kurt headed for the bar and sat alone in a corner, brooding. His muscles vibrated with angry tension and self-disgust. It was true that Mr. Gamble hadn't wanted him to tell Gretchen who he was until Kurt had confirmed her identity and probed her for details that verified she was, indeed, Gamble's daughter, but Kurt didn't like deception and rarely worked cases that called for it. He wished more than ever that he hadn't bent his rigid standards and allowed Gamble to talk him into taking the case.

But he couldn't blame Gamble. The simple fact was that he'd wanted to get to know Gretchen Wagner from the moment he'd first laid eyes on her picture in that *National Geographic* article. He'd been on the verge of refusing the case when the man had slapped the open magazine on Kurt's desk and pointed to Gretchen's picture. He still couldn't explain the certainty that had gripped him, but he'd known immediately that he wanted to find Dr. Gretchen Wagner and meet her face-to-face.

When he finally had, she'd been so sweetly shy that he'd realized immediately she'd clam up when he explained who he was. So he hadn't told her, banking on the attraction between them. He'd hoped against hope that she would be willing to overlook his omission of certain facts because she'd fallen for him as fast as he'd fallen for her.

Holy shit. He'd fallen for her?

Maybe that was too strong. Maybe he was just wildly attracted to her. Yeah, that had to be it.

His chest was tight and he realized he felt oddly panicked. Taking deep, slow breaths, he forced himself to calm down. Attraction could be a powerful force. Just because he was attracted didn't mean he was looking for anything more.

Of course not.

He'd learned his lesson back in Prince George's

County in Maryland. Women were wonderful things if you didn't let yourself get dependent on them.

Straightening his shoulders, he headed for the elevators. He needed a good night's sleep. Then tomorrow he'd plan his next move. But as he shucked off his clothes and headed for a quick shower in his room, he couldn't stop thinking about Gretchen.

She was adopted. No big deal. But when she'd said she was adopted at the age of twelve, he'd been unable to keep from recalling the headlines that had gripped the sleazier papers earlier in the spring.

Apparently, a mistakenly declassified government file recently alluded to a project involving genetic research dating back to the sixties. One tabloid had claimed that the research involved DNA manipulation to produce super people, and that there were several of them running around incognito. Another had stated that the genetically enhanced children had been adopted a little over a decade later when the project was dropped.

Kurt had no idea if there was a single grain of truth in any of the wild claims, but something wouldn't let him dismiss them outright. Gretchen had been adopted at age twelve. She had been a child prodigy of an amazing sort, with her incredible facility for linguistic challenges. Was it possible...?

Nah. He was being as paranoid as the rest of the U.S. population.

In the morning, Kurt got downstairs well ahead of the time Gretchen usually met her young assistant in the lobby. He parked himself in an unobtrusive spot far enough from the elevators that she'd have to get off before she saw him. She'd probably calmed down overnight and thought about what he'd said, and maybe, just maybe, she'd have dinner with him again tonight and let him explain.

An hour after he saw her assistant leave the hotel alone, he was still waiting. Gretchen never appeared.

Hmm. Okay, so maybe she was still a little pissed. And, courtesy of the prodigious brain behind those beautiful blue eyes, she'd realized he'd wait in the lobby so she'd gone another way.

Fine. Two could play that game. Point for point, he was pretty sure her IQ was high enough to put his to shame, but Gretchen wasn't worldly or experienced in surveillance. Figuring out a way to see her should be a piece of cake.

That afternoon, he reluctantly returned a call from Mr. Gamble.

"This is Kurt Miller," he said when the man picked up.

"Miller! Is there a reason you can't seem to keep me informed on a daily basis?" asked Gamble in an icy tone.

"I call when I have something to report," he reminded his employer evenly.

"All right, so report." Gamble's voice turned eager. "Have you spoken to her about me? Set up a meeting?"

"I've told her about you," Kurt said cautiously. "She needs a little time to get used to the idea."

"A little time? How much time?" Gamble demanded. "I don't have time to waste. Did you tell her there's money in it for her?"

Kurt ignored the crass question. "I'll be talking with her again soon, and hopefully I'll have something more concrete for you."

"How soon? Hopefully?" Gamble was practically sputtering. "Dammit, Miller, you came highly recommended. I thought you were supposed to be good at this. If you can't do the job, I'll get someone who can."

"That's your choice, sir. Would you like me to suspend my efforts until you can get hold of another investigator to take over?" Kurt had never responded well to threats, and he laced his voice with a detachment that signaled he'd be more than happy to step away from the case. Even if he was holding his breath, hoping the man didn't call his bluff.

There was a frozen silence from the other end of the line. Finally, Gamble said, "No, that won't be necessary. Just get that girl to agree to meet with me. The sooner the better."

"I'll do that and get back to you later this week." Kurt wasn't about to be pushed around.

Another silence. He thought he heard a muffled conversation, and he suspected Gamble was muting the receiver with his palm. At last the man spoke again. "I'll look forward to hearing from you as soon as possible, Miller."

After concluding the call, Kurt hustled down to the lobby, but Gretchen never came in from outside or appeared for dinner. Shortly before nine, he took the elevator to her floor and strolled past her room as he'd done the day they'd met, pretending that his own lodgings were on the same level. Outside her room was a table on wheels with the remains of a meal.

Damn. He lifted his hand to knock, then hesitated. He'd really hoped to catch her in a public setting, knowing she would be reluctant to create a scene. And now it was growing late and she would be tired and quite possibly even more irritated with him for disturbing her. Much as he loathed the delay, it would be wiser to wait and approach her tomorrow.

He returned to his own room and went to bed. The heck with the public setting. Tomorrow, he'd wait outside her room from six in the morning until midnight if he had to. Gretchen Wagner might think she could evade him but he was patient and determined, and there was no way she could avoid him forever.

Dammit, he missed her.

How could he miss her? He'd only known the woman for three days.

An image of her pretty face framed by thick waves of shining dark hair came to him. She had the deepest blue eyes he'd ever seen. They glowed with intelligence and passion when she was discussing something of interest, so intense that her enthusiasm drew him in as well. Those eyes and dark hair were a striking contrast with her fair skin, touched with a hint of rose in her cheeks that heightened to a warm blush when he teased her.

Last night she'd worn one of his flowers in her hair. She'd worn a long, loose blue dress which flowed and rippled enticingly around her. He was pretty sure she thought it was a modest outfit, but he'd seen the men eyeing her covertly, assessing the soft rise of her breasts and the slim hips that the dress inadvertently enhanced. Those same men had directed their gazes elsewhere after they'd made eye contact with him, he thought with grim satisfaction.

He rose at five-thirty and was outside Gretchen's door by six. There was nowhere to stand or sit that was anything but in-your-face obvious, but he was past caring. He smiled at people as they came out of their rooms and looked at him inquiringly.

"Women," he said to one man, jerking his thumb toward the door.

"I hear you, mate." The accent sounded Australian. "If you're still hanging about later, I'll bring you a plate."

It was the first genuine urge to laugh that he'd had since Gretchen had walked away from him two nights ago.

At ten minutes to nine, Gretchen's door opened and he straightened from his slouch against the wall.

But it wasn't Gretchen who emerged. Instead, it

was a solidly built woman followed by a mousy little man with a Panama hat. The couple started around him and down the hall, and the woman cast him a disapproving look as if he were a Peeping Tom.

"Excuse me." He was completely at sea. "Do you know Gretchen Wagner?"

"I beg your pardon?" the woman asked. "We just flew in yesterday. We've hardly had time to make acquaintances."

He pondered the words. "You arrived yesterday...and were assigned to this room?"

The man nodded. The woman took him by the arm. "Who are you?" she asked. "Is there a reason you're interrogating us?"

"I was just looking for a friend," Kurt said. "Apparently I have the wrong room."

"Apparently you do." The couple turned and headed down the hallway, and Kurt followed more slowly.

He was starting to get seriously annoyed. Little sneak. He couldn't help but admire the way she'd outfoxed him, even if he was madder than hell. She must have switched rooms, anticipating his determination to talk further with her.

He had breakfast and spent the day sightseeing. He'd done tours of the Pyramids of Giza, the islands of Gezira and Roda and the Egyptian museum already, so he joined a guided tour that focused on the architecture of the city with its Islamic influences, minarets and carved domes and its medieval buildings dating back over a thousand years. It was a fascinating tour and under any other circumstances he'd have been wrapped up in the information, but today he couldn't concentrate on anything the guide was saying.

Midway through the afternoon, he slipped away from the tour and headed back to the hotel. At the desk, he asked the clerk for Gretchen's room number but, as he'd expected, was denied.

"I'm sorry, sir, but we never reveal our guests' room numbers. Would you like to leave a message for her?"

"Yes," he said.

The clerk punched in her name, but a moment later he had a puzzled look on his face. "I have no Gretchen Wagner registered. Could you spell that last name for me?"

A few minutes later, Kurt was convinced that Gretchen was no longer staying in the hotel—at least under her own name. And he doubted she had the fake ID or the chutzpah to register under an alias. Which meant she really had checked out.

Panic rose. Had she returned to the States? He thought for a moment, forcing himself to think logically. Recalling the animation that had lit her lovely features when she spoke of her work on the Ahk Tablets, he felt the vise squeezing his heart ease a little. Gretchen was committed to that project. He knew her well enough to be sure that she wouldn't walk away until it was complete.

Reassured, he got a cool drink and waited in the lobby, sifting through his options and deciding on his next move. He could begin by calling every hotel in the area, but there was an easier method he wanted to try first. At approximately five-fifteen, just as he'd hoped, Gretchen's assistant breezed in through the revolving lobby doors.

He stood, quickly crossing to intercept her before she got into an elevator. "Excuse me," he said, "but do you work with Gretchen Wagner?"

The girl studied him for a minute, then grinned hugely. "Yeah, and you're the hunk she met in the elevator that she got all dressed up for the other night, right?"

He had to chuckle. "Yes to the elevator, anyway."

She cocked her head. "I'm Nancy," she announced, offering her hand.

"Kurt Miller." He returned the courtesy. "I'm trying to get in touch with Gretchen. Could you give me any pointers?"

"Why?" She was still friendly, but cautious, as he'd anticipated.

He decided honesty might be the best policy in this case—at least partial honesty. And just in case, he turned the charm up another notch. "We were getting to know each other and we had a misunderstanding the other night. I need to apologize." He forced himself to smile. "I know she moved to another hotel and I'd like to surprise her with an apology and some flowers. Do you think she'll forgive me?"

Six

Early the next morning he rehearsed different ways to approach her as he walked to the Nile Hilton, another large cosmopolitan hotel in the westernized district near Midan Tehrir. It was a relief to know that she hadn't fled the country entirely, although he'd suspected as much. Still, she was a woman, and he'd never pretended to understand the way a woman's mind worked.

Thanks to her assistant, Nancy, Kurt knew her room number and was able to go straight up. He knocked on the door, then stepped to one side so she couldn't see him, knowing that the element of surprise was on his side.

"Who is it?" Her clear tones floated through the door.

"Message for Ms. Wagner." He did his best with an Arabic accent.

When she opened the door, there was a pleasant, questioning expression on her face. When she saw him, her smile disappeared and her fair skin flushed. She immediately attempted to shut the door, but he blocked it simply by putting his palm against it.

"You have every right to be angry with me," Kurt said quickly, "but I have a job to do. I can't force you to do anything you don't want to do, but I have a responsibility to my client to present you with all the facts." He'd decided the business approach was the best start. Then he could work on repairing their personal relationship.

"Your client." Her tone was bitter. "Who expects me to believe he's my long-lost father."

"The sooner you listen to what I have to say, the sooner you can get me to go away." Although he was hoping that he could change her mind about that.

She studied him for a long moment, her eyes blank and unreadable, and then she raised her hands in resignation. "All right. You may as well come in." As she led the way into her suite and indicated that he should take a seat, she said, "How did you find me? I assumed you'd think I'd left Egypt."

"You wouldn't leave without finishing the job you agreed to do," he said confidently. He moved to the seat she indicated but remained standing.

She looked a little taken aback, then she nodded. "You're right."

There was a small silence while she looked at him expectantly, and he realized he was going to have to explain himself. He'd been hoping he wouldn't have to reveal her assistant's indiscretion. He didn't want to get the girl fired. "Nancy told me," he said, "but don't blame her. She's a romantic and she thinks we had a lovers' quarrel."

Gretchen finally appeared to see that he was waiting for her to take a seat and she lowered herself to the couch opposite him with an uncharacteristically harsh laugh. "You sure fooled her."

"Gretchen, I—"

"Don't." Her voice was sharp and she held up a hand, palm out in command. "Do not start with anything personal or I'll call Security and have you thrown out. Just tell me what you need to tell me and then go."

She wasn't kidding, he could read it in the set expression on her face, and his heart sank. He hadn't expected this to be easy—well, maybe he had, a little—but right now he felt as if he'd be lucky to ever get a smile out of her again. No, seeing one of those warm, special smiles she'd showered on him before he'd told her the truth was probably as likely as seeing a living dinosaur. Damn. He was no Casanova, but he knew how to be charming and he'd used it before to overcome a woman's hesitations. He supposed it had been stupidly arrogant of him to assume that Gretchen could be manipulated that way. It served him right. But telling himself that didn't make it any easier to swallow.

She was looking at him expectantly, almost challengingly. Forcing himself to set aside his frustration and disappointment, he told himself that at least he was in the same room with her. It could have been worse. She could have slammed the door in his face.

"All right," he said slowly.

He reached into his jacket and withdrew a small handheld computer in which he kept information. The little unit interfaced with his home computer, storing everything he put into it. Using a special stylus, he pulled up the file on Oliver Gamble and consulted his notes. "Gamble believes you are his daughter for a number of reasons. First, you look exactly like his deceased wife, according to him."

"How would he know what I look like?"

"*National Geographic,*" he said succinctly.

"Oh. I forgot. Is that how he found me?"

"I believe that may be what caught his attention initially," Kurt admitted. "The more he learned, the more convinced he became." He glanced at his notes again, though he knew them by heart. "He says that his daughter was born in November of 1967. When's your birthday?"

Gretchen had lost the high color she'd had when she'd tried to throw him out. Her face was pale now, and at his words, she lost what little rosy hue she'd had left. "I don't know. Only the year—1967—was listed on the adoption papers. My parents always celebrated it on February fourteenth." A sad smile tugged at the corners of her mouth but died before it grew into happiness. "They always said I was the best Valentine they ever got."

He wanted to comfort her, but she'd probably take his hand off at the wrist if he tried. Kurt turned his handheld computer around to show her his notes, using the opportunity to lean closer to her as he did so.

"He also claims that his daughter spoke five languages fluently before she was twelve."

"Five languages." It was almost a whisper. "English, Spanish, French..."

"...Japanese and Italian." He finished the list with her.

Her eyes were haunted. "What else?"

"He and his wife had been told their daughter was a child prodigy in anything to do with linguistics, that they should consider accelerating her education because she'd be bored silly in a regular school. He told me that she should be given as much special instruction in languages, linguistics, literature and semantics as possible because she had the most extraordinary capabilities of anyone the teachers and doctors had ever seen."

"Just like me." He got the feeling she was talking to herself. Then she shook her head. "All right, there are a lot of similarities. I'll grant you that. But that's all they are." She sounded desperate to convince him. Or herself. "Similarities that are sheer coincidence. There must be millions of dark-haired, blue-eyes girls born in November of 1967."

"And how many of them do you think spoke five languages at the age of twelve? How many graduated years ahead of their peers? How many," he pressed, "are professors who specialize like you do and hold prestigious positions at Ivy League schools?"

Gretchen was silent. He could feel her resistance as surely as if it were a wall standing before him.

"Why are you so determined not to consider the possibility that at least one of your biological parents is alive?" He couldn't keep the touch of exasperation from his tone. "Doesn't the thought of finding—"

"No!" She cut him off before he could even finish the thought. "I'm *not* thrilled by the thought. I told you about my missing memories," she said, and there was a combative, accusatory tone in her voice now. "Hasn't it occurred to you that my parents probably have something to do with that? What kind of trauma was I subjected to before they shipped me off to the highest bidder?"

"You don't know that's what happened."

"My parents—my *real* parents—were extremely wealthy. They were both well over forty when I was adopted. Even you probably know enough about adoption laws to know how unusual that is. Smells like there was money involved to me."

"There's money involved in every adoption."

"Not the kind of money I suspect changed hands in mine. And besides, even if it wasn't a crooked deal, how do you explain my memory loss? People don't just go around forgetting their entire childhoods."

"True," he said, "but to assume your biological parents had something to do with it is a bit of a stretch."

She looked mulish. "Not to me."

"For all we know," he pointed out, "you could have been the subject of a custody battle. Maybe your mother took you away from your father. Maybe that's where this trauma that affected your recall occurred.''

''Did he tell you that?'' Her voice was suspicious.

Kurt shook his head. ''The only things he's ever said about your mother are that you resemble her and that she's deceased. I only said it to make you see how many possibilities there are.''

Gretchen heaved a sigh rife with frustration. ''All right. Assume I agree to meet him. What does he want?''

''He wants to get to know you. I think I told you he's wealthy. He has no other heirs.''

She looked incredulous. ''And he thinks I would accept his money?''

''Lots of people would be thrilled to be in this situation,'' he said truthfully.

''I'm not lots of people.''

He had to smile. ''No, you certainly aren't.''

She didn't smile back. ''What else?''

He shrugged. ''Are you willing to talk with the man?''

She hesitated. But as she opened her mouth to respond, an ear-splitting siren began to shriek.

They both jumped.

''Fire alarm,'' he shouted over the din. ''We'll have to evacuate.''

''Fire?'' He could hear a hysterical note of panic in her voice even over the deafening effects of the siren. ''Oh, God, fire. What do we do? How will we get out?''

He reached out and grabbed her wrist, starting for the door. ''Come on. There's an evacuation plan right here on the back of the door.''

But she was resisting and when he glanced back, he was startled to see her sink to her knees. Her chest was heaving with rapid, shallow breaths, and he knew she would pass out if she didn't calm down and get more air.

''Come on,'' he repeated. He turned and scooped her up in his arms.

Immediately she threw her arms around his neck in a stranglehold so tight he thought for a minute she might just choke him. She buried her head in his neck, and against his broad chest, he could feel her slender frame trembling violently.

He threw open the door and moved down the hall with a stream of other hotel guests who were rushing like lemmings toward the emergency exits. The evacuation was hasty but orderly, thanks to a number of calm employees who held open the stairwell doors and cautioned people not to panic.

As they descended the second set of steps, she stirred in his arms. ''I can walk.'' Her voice was less panicked, but when he set her on her feet, she clutched at his arms. ''Please don't leave me.''

''I won't.'' He swept an arm around her waist, holding her close to his side. ''You're safe with me,'' he promised her, feeling a rather primitive satisfaction in her apparent dependence on him.

Gretchen's room had only been on the seventh

floor, and in a matter of minutes, they were striding out into the blinding Egyptian early-morning sunshine in a horde of milling, babbling tourists in various stages of dress.

When they reached a safe distance and there were no longer emergency personnel urging them to keep moving, Kurt slowed, pulling Gretchen to a stop beside him. He turned and looked at the hotel, seeing no evidence of smoke or fire yet.

"It's probably a false alarm," he said soothingly to her, keeping her within the circle of his arms. "I've had it happen a number of times while I'm traveling. You'll be allowed to go back in a little bit, I bet."

She lay against him, unresisting, a stark contrast to the rigidly angry woman he'd been facing just minutes ago. "Will you come with me?"

"Of course." He put a hand to her cheek and tilted her face up so that he could see her eyes. "Are you all right?"

"No." Her tone was flat, defeated. "I'm sorry. Ever since I can remember, I've been terribly afraid of fire. There are so many things that can explode when there's a fire—"

Her voice was rising and he cut her off with a finger against her lips. "Shh. You're all right now. Nothing's going to happen." He palmed the back of her head and pressed her close, and she snuggled in against him like she belonged there.

It felt startlingly right, and for a moment he simply

let himself savor the sweetness of the embrace. After the depth of the anger he'd seen in her, he'd been afraid he might have ruined any chance with her.

But then his mind clicked into gear again. Her reaction to the mere possibility of a fire was way out of proportion. What would she do if she actually saw flames or smelled smoke?

He felt incredibly protective, and he had to remind himself that she'd all but thrown him out of her room earlier. Once things were restored to normal, he could kiss this temporary closeness goodbye.

Suddenly, she stiffened against him. "What's wrong?" he asked.

"An explosion." Her voice was soft, her eyes faraway as she pulled back to look up at him. "I can see it in my head!" Her voice became animated, breathless with a child's remembered fear. "The boat was burning. There was fire coming out of the portholes and all of sudden...all of a sudden, the whole thing just blew apart! It just blew apart," she repeated.

He was stunned. "You're sure it's a memory? What else? Was there anyone with you? Who was on the boat?"

She stood perfectly still in his arms, her attention turned inward as she fought to recall more. But finally she sagged in defeat. "I don't know," she admitted. "I can see the boat, and the way it blew up, quite clearly. But I can't tell where I was, or who I might have been with... But I don't think I was alone.'' She expelled a breath and he could hear the frustration in it. ''It's like it's right there beyond the tips of my fingers but I can't quite grasp it. I'm almost positive it's not just something I saw in a movie.'' She paused, clearly groping for the right words. ''It feels...personal. God, I wish I could remember more.''

''Don't try to push it,'' he advised. ''Everything I've ever heard about amnesia says that your memory will return in its own good time, if at all. You can't make it happen.''

''I know. Don't you think I've tried?'' She sounded so forlorn.

He rubbed her back, and she lay her head against his shoulder again. ''It's all right, Professor.''

''Kurt?''

''Yes?''

''Do you believe your client really is my father?''

''I don't know. But I think the possibility is strong enough that it might be worth checking out further.''

''All right.''

All right? Had she just agreed with him? Whimsically, he looked at the sky as if lightning might strike.

Then the emergency workers began to recall the people standing on the sidewalk. As he escorted Gretchen past them, he heard, ''...small grease fire in the kitchen...easily contained...''

At the door of her room, he prepared to leave her. As he said goodbye, she put her hand on his arm.

"Wait," she said.

He turned back.

"Could we have dinner tonight—or tomorrow night, if you're busy this evening? I'd like to talk further with you about your client."

He nodded. "I don't have any other plans tonight," he said gently. Had she really thought he would give up that easily? "How about I pick you up at six?"

"All right." She squeezed his arm and offered him a tentative smile. "Thank you. I'm sorry I was such a baby."

He shrugged, smiling at her. "My pleasure. I'm glad I was here."

"I'm glad you were, too," she said soberly.

Back at the hotel, Kurt phoned his employer. "I need some details," he told Oliver Gamble.

"Details? Of what?" The man's voice was testy. "Once she and I meet, I can give her all the details she wants."

"She's not sure she wants to meet you," Kurt said baldly.

"What?" It was an explosive exclamation. "She has to!"

"No, sir, she doesn't. But I think she'll be willing if she isn't rushed."

Silence. Kurt waited through it with admirable patience.

Finally Gamble spoke. "What do you want to know?"

"You say her mother isn't living?"

"No. She, ah, died a few years ago."

"Siblings?"

"I've told you," Gamble said tersely. "She's an only child."

Kurt thought for a moment. "Where did she grow up?"

"The Southeast."

"Would she ever have been to a beach?"

"Yes. We lived quite near one." Gamble was feeding him oddly generalized information, it seemed to Kurt. Though he couldn't put a finger on it, something about the man's responses bothered him.

"Care to be more specific?"

"No." Gamble sounded as if he might be gritting his teeth. "I thought you said she'd lost her memory of her life with us. If that's true, maybe it's not a good idea to be overwhelming her with a lot of information. I believe I'll call a psychologist and ask about memory disorders."

"All right. How would you like me to proceed?"

"I want to meet her as soon as possible. Arrange it."

"I'll do my best. Mr. Gamble?"

"What?"

"You've said Gretchen resembles her mother?" She certainly didn't resemble Gamble in any way.

"Yes." He sighed, as if reluctant to rehash this

line of questioning. "Gretchen looked a great deal like her as a child and from what I saw in that *National Geographic* article I showed you, she still does. Her mother has the same striking dark blue eyes."

Has? A chill slithered down Kurt's spine. Gamble had clearly stated that Gretchen's mother was dead. Maybe it was just a slip of the tongue. That was probably it. Maybe.

He concluded the call and hung up thoughtfully. The bad feeling was back, stronger than ever. He'd learned to heed it well during the years when trusting his intuition could have meant life or death. So what was there about Oliver Gamble that was giving him the feeling that something wasn't quite right? Maybe he should consider trying to confirm the veracity of the man's interest in Gretchen.

Especially since he couldn't get that story about genetically enhanced adopted children out of his head.

Picking up the phone, he placed a second call to the States. His old friend Aiden Swift was out of the business now, happily married to the woman he'd let get away once before, but a man with Aiden's past was never completely outside the loop. He wanted to know everything of public record about Oliver Gamble.

Aiden wasn't home. He left a message, hoping his friend wasn't out of the country. He'd give him two weeks and then try again when he got back to the States if he hadn't checked in by then.

Seven

The Egyptian Museum where the work on the Ahk Tablets was being conducted was so close to Gretchen's new hotel that she made it back to her room in plenty of time for a leisurely bath, even though she'd worked late again. Actually, she'd forced herself to stay through the afternoon, although she couldn't honestly claim to have gotten a lot of work done.

Angry as she had been—and still was—at Kurt's deliberate deception, he made her feel safe and protected in a way she'd never experienced before. Added to the unbelievable sex appeal the man exuded, it was a powerful combination.

A combination she had to resist. How could she possibly trust him after this?

After her bath, she dressed in the sleeveless, short black cocktail dress she'd bought and worn the other night. Since they weren't leaving the hotel, she could wear it in relative comfort, though she'd become so used to wearing long, modest styles that she felt terribly exposed.

You've been working in Egypt too long, she told herself.

Besides, she wanted to look nice tonight. Angry at him though she still was, Kurt Miller appealed to her. He drew her physically, as well as with his logical intellect and his sense of humor, the integrity that shone from his brown eyes—integrity she *thought* she'd seen in his eyes, she corrected herself. He'd told her he wanted to see her when they returned to the States. He'd told her he was attracted to her: *"I've never met a woman I like as much as I like you before."* He'd led her to believe that he felt their budding relationship was as special as she had thought it was. *"When we danced last night...well, I'm hoping you recognized how special it was, too."*

Had that all been part of the act to get into her good graces before he shared his real purpose with her? She couldn't think of any reason that he would have had to go to those lengths. After all, she'd already been putty in his hands by then. Was she a fool for thinking that there'd been something genuine in his voice when he'd said, *"I wanted to hold you in my arms one more time before you kicked my teeth out?"*

Maybe.

Probably.

But she still couldn't completely squelch the hope that leaped inside her when she saw him standing at the corner of the elevator bank waiting for her.

"Hi," he said. His voice was husky and there was

something almost vulnerable in his tone. "There's a good Italian restaurant here if you're interested. If not, there's a bigger place with a variety of American food."

"No," she said, "Italian would be fine."

He took her elbow and turned her in the direction he wanted her to walk, and the touch of his fingers on her bare skin sent licks of flame through her. "I like that dress. I'm glad you wore it again." His voice was low and warm and when she glanced up, he was looking down at her with an obvious hunger in his eyes.

She looked away quickly, torn between wanting to feed that hunger and wanting to keep her distance, to salvage her dignity and her heart from his deception. "Thank you."

They headed for the restaurant and were seated, then Kurt ordered a bottle of full-bodied red wine. As soon as the sommelier left, Kurt said, "I spoke with my employer after I left you this morning."

"Oh?"

"He gave me a few details to share with you."

She couldn't prevent herself from leaning forward eagerly. "Tell me."

"He said you look like your mother." He swirled the wine in his glass, holding it up to the light and looking at the ruby liquid with assessing eyes.

"You told me that before. Did he tell you her name?"

He shook his head.

"What's *his* name?"

"Gamble. Oliver Gamble. He also said your mother passed away a few years ago." He frowned.

"What?"

Kurt shook his head. "Nothing."

"One thing I don't understand," she said.

He lifted an eyebrow in silent inquiry.

"If he knew who I was and where I worked, why didn't he come to Egypt himself? Is he very old, or ill?"

Kurt shook his head. "Neither, as far as I know. In fact, I asked him something similar when he hired me and he said he had a number of irons in the fire and that he couldn't just take off at the present time. A lot of people use intermediaries for initial contact with a birth relative," he said, trying to cast Gamble's behavior in a positive light as a matter of fairness.

Now it was her turn to frown as she considered the information. "Oliver Gamble," she said slowly. "Gretchen Gamble." She shook her head and her eyes were troubled. "It doesn't ring any bells. It doesn't even feel...right."

Kurt only watched her with enigmatic eyes.

"But then again, I've thought of myself as Gretchen Wagner for all of the years I *can* remember. Maybe that's all it is—" Suddenly she broke off, putting a hand to her head.

She was on the beach, running along the edge of the tide line. It was a hot, sunny day but there was a delightful light breeze blowing in off the sea and the dull roar of the breaking waves was punctuated by the occasional screech from a seagull.

This memory, or whatever it was, was far more vivid and detailed than any she'd ever had before.

Farther up the beach the sand was so hot it burned her feet, but down here next to the water it held the blurred outline of her small footprints for a sluggish moment until the next incoming wavelet lapped over it, erasing any sign that she'd been there.

The tide was out and she skidded to a halt as she nearly ran over a sand dollar newly cast upon the shore. It was large, grayish-lavender and complete, not a chipped edge in sight. Those were hard to find! She snatched it up, proud and excited.

"What do you have there, honey?"

Some distance down the sand, her mother stood waiting, laughing, arms outstretched. She ran as fast as her little legs would carry her, giggling as she went. "Mama!"

Her mother caught her close as she flung herself the last few steps into those arms, smoothing back the dark hair from her daughter's forehead. "I love you," she said, her blue eyes dark with emotion.

"Gretchen?" She became aware that Kurt was holding both her hands in a grip so tight it nearly hurt.

"I...I remember her," she whispered. She squeezed his fingers tightly. "I remember my mother!"

"Tell me."

"I was little. Running along a beach. It was summertime, or somewhere tropical because it was hot and sunny. The sand was very white, and I found a sand dollar." She paused and met his eyes. "My mother was waiting for me. She hugged me and it was almost as if I could feel her arms around me."

"How do you know it was your mother?" She glared at him and he smiled. "Just playing devil's advocate."

"I don't know how I know," she admitted. "But it *was*. She had dark hair and blue eyes and...I do look a lot like her!" she said dazedly. After so many years of having no memories at all, this was overwhelming.

Kurt scooted his chair halfway around the little table to her side. He put an arm around her and squeezed gently. "That's terrific," he said sincerely. "Your father said you lived in the Southeast, quite near a beach. So what you just recalled must be a true memory."

But she frowned a little. "That's not quite right," she said slowly. "We lived...right on the beach. I'm sure of it. Our house was big." She looked up at him, a bit shocked. "Our house was *huge!* It was like one of those antebellum mansions that makes you think of the pre-Civil War South. You could see it from the beach," she told Kurt.

"Could it have been a vacation home?"

She hesitated, trying to force more of her past to

the surface, but finally she sighed in frustration. "I don't know for sure, but I don't think so. Something about it seems...permanent." Then she said, "What are you doing?"

He had pulled one of his business cards from his pocket, turned it over and was scribbling on the back. "Writing it down exactly the way you said it. Now that you've remembered, I doubt you'll forget it again, but just in case the memory doesn't stay clear..."

He was so thoughtful. "Thank you. That's a good idea." Then she began to sift through the memories running through her mind. They were sharp and clear, as if they'd just happened yesterday. But they ended abruptly, leaving her with the feeling that there was more, much more, if she could only unlock some door in her mind.

"I don't remember my father," she said.

Kurt stopped writing and laid the card aside as the waiter came with their meals. "He probably worked and wasn't around as much." He shrugged. "I'd think it was normal for a small child's primary memories to be of the mother."

As they began to eat, he went on to tell her about some of the tours he had taken while in Cairo, and she was warmed by his consideration as she realized that he was deliberately chattering casually, giving her time to examine the new additions to her past.

When the meal was finished, they left the restaurant. She picked up the card on which he'd been writing and skimmed her own words as they walked out into the large lobby of the hotel. Idly, she flipped it over, absently reading the inscription. *Kurt J. Miller. Licensed Private Investigator.* He certainly was discreet—

And suddenly another fragment of memory came shooting out of the recesses of her mind. *J...J...Jay?* An image sprang full-blown into her head, a dark-haired boy in a grimy T-shirt, beaming, standing beside an intricate tower of children's interlocking building pieces that was nearly as tall as he was. He was...he was...he was her brother!

"I had a brother," she blurted, astonished at the rush of memory. "His name was Jay, I think. Did my father say anything about him?"

Kurt hesitated, and she knew the answer before he spoke. "No. I'm sorry. I don't have any information about a brother. According to your father, you're an only child."

"I did have a brother," she insisted. She concentrated, again trying to force the memory out of hiding as she'd never done before, but all she encountered was a blank wall.

"I believe you." Kurt hesitated, drawing her to a halt beside a large column. "Maybe something happened to him."

"You mean...he died." The bright flare of excitement the moment of recall had brought fled and a desolation stronger than anything she'd known since her parents had died filled her. Turning away from Kurt, she blinked back hot tears.

"Hey." Kurt's voice was low and soft. His hands were gentle as he turned her around and drew her in against him, and the sheer rightness she felt as their bodies fit together took her breath away. "I'll ask your father about it again."

"What if I had a brother who died?" She was too tired of hurting to mask her pain. "I couldn't bear it if I remember him and he's dead," she said against his chest.

One big hand cradled her jaw and he slipped a thumb beneath her chin to lift her face to his. "Shh. It'll be all right." And then he bent his head and kissed her.

It was as heady and heavenly as she remembered from their first night together. He explored her mouth thoroughly, holding her firmly against him. He'd lied to her, or at the very least, omitted some important information when they'd first met. And yet she felt a deep certainty, a rightness that she didn't fully understand but felt compelled to heed, that told her that this was the man she'd waited for all those lonely years.

He lifted his mouth from hers and their foreheads touched as he bent his head. His chest rose and fell heavily as he said, "We'll work this out. I promise."

She wasn't sure if he was referring to their mutual attraction or the situation with her father, but with his use of the word "we," she felt a reassuring warmth. She was more to him than just another client. She knew it.

Kurt met her for breakfast early the next morning, then walked with her to the museum. Cairo was a study in contrasting architecture. The light-colored adobe buildings almost glowing in the early morning light posed a jarring contrast to the modern, squared-off office complexes. Along the far side of the street a man led a cow while taxis and cars whizzed past him, honking madly. A fine mix of sand and dust filled the air, making Gretchen glad for the enveloping clothing she wore.

Kurt's tall form shadowed hers and she felt both vulnerable and protected at the same time. She truly understood, for the first time, why females throughout history chose the strongest and most powerful males to be their mates.

They reached the entrance to the museum then, and Kurt stopped. "Have you given any more thought to meeting your father?"

An odd sensation gripped her, almost as if she couldn't get enough air. "No," she said. "I haven't."

"He's anxious to meet you as soon as possible."

She felt anxious, too, but not for the same reason, she was sure. "I have at least two more weeks of work ahead of me before I wrap up this project," she said, and was immediately appalled at herself. That was a blatant lie; she'd been making plans to finish within the next few days. Unobtrusively, she tried to inhale deeply.

Kurt whistled. ''Two weeks? Mr. Gamble would like you to come back to the States tomorrow, if possible.''

She shook her head. ''I can't—'' She broke off, gasping for air as she put a hand to her chest. It felt as though a giant hand was compressing her lungs. ''Sorry,'' she managed. ''I need air.''

Kurt hustled her through the massive arched entrance of the building. He was stopped for a security check and she leaned heavily against the wall while he was searched, feeling fine tremors of anxiety shaking her. Once inside the atrium, she sank onto a nearby stone bench.

''Sorry,'' she wheezed. ''I just felt like I couldn't catch my breath.''

Kurt regarded her for a moment. ''Have you ever had panic attacks?''

The unexpected question threw her. ''No,'' she said indignantly. ''I'm not the nervous type.''

''I didn't think you were.'' He took her hand again. ''But given the stress that remembering your past might be placing on you, it's not impossible. What happened just now certainly looked like one to me.''

''And you're an expert?''

''A former client had them frequently,'' he said quietly.

Gretchen closed her eyes. She couldn't deal with

any of this. Especially not meeting her father. At the mere thought, the air suddenly felt closer.

"You could be right," she conceded, striving for a professional tone. "Who knows what's buried in my subconscious? There could be a good reason for the way I'm feeling."

Kurt nodded. "How about if I tell Mr. Gamble that you won't be back for at least two weeks and that we'll contact him when you return and settle in?"

She felt an enormous sense of relief. "That would be wonderful." It was only two weeks. So why did it feel like a reprieve from the guillotine? Quickly, she reviewed her timeline. She didn't have to rush back to the U.S. And no one would ever know if she stretched out her project a bit. Nancy, however, had had her fill of Egypt; perhaps Gretchen would send her home tomorrow. That would make it easier to look busy for two weeks.

He took Gretchen to breakfast and dinner every night for the next three days. Nancy went home and as the days passed, he sensed Gretchen relaxing. She smiled more easily and laughed frequently. Her face radiated happiness, and he was deeply pleased that he seemed to be the cause of her pleasure.

The only concern he noted was the fact that anytime he mentioned her father, Gretchen immediately tensed up and her face became the inanimate mask she was so adept at wearing. Why would the mere mention of finding her biological father cause such a reaction? He didn't know, but he kept thinking that there must be a good reason.

When he had called to tell Gamble that Gretchen still had two weeks' work in Cairo, the man's reaction had been completely outside what Kurt considered normal bounds, so angry that Kurt had again suggested Gamble hire a new PI. He was beginning to feel so strongly about it that he'd actually considered returning his retainer and never putting the two in touch at all. Was it intuition warning him or was it simply his ridiculous imagination?

Just as he was beginning to wonder if Gamble was lying about Gretchen's lack of siblings. Unfortunately, he hadn't even gotten to ask about it before Gamble went ballistic. He thought of Aiden Swift and wondered when he might hear something about Gamble. Last night he'd called another old friend as well, for assistance of a different kind.

Jared Sullivan also was a former client. Or at least, indirectly so. Six years ago, Kurt had been hired to find him and give him news of a significant inheritance. In the process, he'd grown to like the reserved former special ops soldier. He'd attended his wedding recently, and thoroughly approved of Jared's bride, Dr. Alexis Warner, an amazing woman in her own right.

Both Jared and his new bride were special agents. Kurt was counting on them to look into the not-so-public records that Aiden probably couldn't get at. The concerns niggling at the corners of his mind weren't going to go away until he was certain Gamble was nothing more than an overly anxious father.

He'd even gone so far as to send Jared and Alex one of Gretchen's hair bands that she'd mislaid, complete with clinging hairs, and a manila envelope Gamble had given him. It was one of the standard glue kind, and he had watched Gamble lick the flap himself at his office in Texas, so he was hoping Jared could pull some strings and get a DNA cross-check for him.

But all that took time. Opening information sources that were supposed to be secure sometimes took a bit of finesse, too, but he knew Jared could do it.

On his fourth afternoon with Gretchen, he suggested they go swimming before the sun set in the late evening. He left her at the door to her room and went to his own, now in this hotel to which he'd moved. After changing into swim trunks, he returned for her.

When they arrived at the pool, she made a beeline for one of the poolside lounge chairs. "I'm not in the mood to swim but I'll be happy to keep you company."

"What?" He thought she might be kidding, except that Gretchen rarely made jokes. "Come on, it'll be great."

She shook her head again. "No, really. You go ahead. I'll just sit here and get some sun."

He cocked his head, studying her. Although she'd

sat down in the lounge chair, she hadn't removed the casual, flowing dress she'd worn over her suit, and she was sitting bolt upright with the rigid posture of someone ready to leap to her feet and flee any second. What could be bothering her? "You're not going to get much sun that way."

She glanced down at herself, and he could see a blush rising into her cheeks. She twisted her fingers together, a mannerism he'd noticed emerged whenever she was uncomfortable or upset. "You're right."

She looked reluctant as she stood and slipped the dress off, then quickly sat back down again.

He didn't speak for a minute. Instead, he turned and dove into the pool, breaking the surface and circling back to where she sat. The water felt good; it was surprisingly cool. And that wasn't a bad thing, he decided wryly, given the irrepressible arousal that the sight of her caused.

The suit she wore was modest by American standards. It was a dark indigo tankini that complemented her glossy dark hair and contrasted with her fair skin. The neck was slightly scooped and the bottom half covered her more than adequately.

Still, he was mesmerized. Her figure was so slender he suspected his hands might span her waist, and her well-muscled legs looked a mile long. The small part of his brain that was still working wondered if she did a lot of walking back in the States.

Hastily, he turned back into the pool and did a

powerful crawl around the enormous space for ten minutes or so. Finally, when he was firmly in possession of his self-control, he swam back to where she sat.

Crossing his arms on the lip of the pool, he floated there near the foot of her chair and studied her openly. A possibility occurred to him. "Gretchen," he said gently, "do you know how to swim?"

She sat up even straighter, if that was possible. "Of course I can swim. I just don't care to, that's all."

"You don't care to?"

A visible shudder ran over her. "No."

"When was the last time you went swimming?"

She stared at him. The silence between them lengthened, but he held her gaze until she slowly shook her head, her expression troubled. "I don't remember. I don't think I've ever gone swimming since I was adopted."

"So how do you know you can swim?"

"We swam in the ocean all the time when I was little. Mom made sure all of us could swim."

He felt a frisson of shock run down his spine. She didn't even seem to realize what she'd said, so he asked another quiet question. "Who went swimming with you?"

"My parents and my brothers and my sister." Then she drew in a quick, sharp breath, almost a sob. "Kurt! Did you hear what I said?"

He nodded. He boosted himself out of the pool and

sat beside her, dripping wet, because she looked so shocked and vulnerable he couldn't stand it. "I heard you." He dried himself haphazardly with one of the towels the hotel provided, then put an arm around her. "Do you remember anything else?"

She shook her head wildly. "No. Yes! I had three brothers and a sister." She looked up at him. "I have siblings out there somewhere, don't I?"

He nodded. "Possibly." *So why did Gamble keep telling him Gretchen was an only child?* "I don't know a lot about amnesia but I don't think people generally manufacture fake memories of old events."

"Oh, God." She put a shaking hand over her eyes. "I feel like I'm going crazy. Why would my father lie to me?"

Kurt didn't have an answer for that one. "I don't know but let's not leap to conclusions. Maybe there's a perfectly reasonable explanation." *Right. And maybe it would snow in Cairo tomorrow.*

Eight

"Why don't I take you to your room?" Kurt put his own shirt and shoes on, then helped her to her feet and slipped her dress over her head. After she stepped into her sandals, he led her back through the hotel to the elevators that took them to her floor. Gretchen merely stood at his side like a mannequin the entire time, moving only when his hand on her elbow urged her forward.

When he opened her room door, he gestured for her to precede him, then followed her in and let the door shut behind him. "Gretchen?"

She turned slowly, and when she met his eyes, her own were dull with anxiety. "I'll be all right," she said in a monotone.

He was willing to bet that was a lie, so he ignored her words and crossed the room, drawing her into his arms. "It's okay to cry," he murmured, rubbing her back.

"I don't want to cry," she muttered against his chest. "I want to *remember.*"

For a long moment, there was silence in the room, broken only by the light sound of their breathing.

Kurt stroked her back and skimmed his hand lightly over her dark hair. "You'll remember when you're ready to," he finally said.

Gretchen drew away from him a little. "You must think I'm a pitiful thing," she said. "Afraid of fire, afraid of water, panic attacks, can't remember a third of my life..." She laughed but the sound was bitter. "Believe it or not, I was self-sufficient, well-organized and reasonably unflappable until I started having these memory flashes."

"Until I came along." The realization made him wince.

She looked shocked. "Oh, I'm not blaming you. You're just the messenger." She took a deep breath. "You've been much kinder than I suspect many people would have been."

"Kindness isn't what's motivating me." He leaned forward and brushed his mouth lightly along her temple. What a dumb thing that had been to say, he berated himself. The last thing he wanted her to think was that he was being nice to her to get her to sleep with him. Sure, he'd die a happy man if he ever got her into his bed, but that wasn't what he'd meant.

He couldn't examine the words too closely. Exactly what *had* he meant? He hoped like hell she didn't ask him.

Gretchen was still gazing up at him, a puzzled frown on her face. When she frowned, her full lower lip pouted in what he could only say was an incredibly erotic way, and he struggled to resist the urge to bend and put his mouth over hers.

Instead, he drew her with him to the love seat and sat down. She needed comfort right now, not a sex-crazed maniac. He patted his knees. "Here. Sit down."

Gretchen looked at him doubtfully. "I'm too heavy."

He laughed. "I could hold two of you. Come here."

She angled herself and sat reluctantly, perching gingerly on his knees. She was so clearly uncomfortable that he was abruptly reminded of her unusual past. For the first time he began to understand what her adolescence must have been like.

He still wasn't quite sure what to say to her about his motivations, but he knew he couldn't leave it hanging as he had. Slowly he said, "I'm sorry that your life has been altered this way. It must have been difficult enough to find yourself a young teenager with new parents and no idea of what had happened to your old family. Anyone would find it unpleasant to have it all dredged up again."

She nodded. "Today at work I had a lot of trouble concentrating." She smiled wryly. "It's a good thing I have most of this project completed."

He was gazing at her mouth, at the way her lips quirked up at one corner a bit more than the other, at the dimple that appeared in her left cheek when she smiled. It was an effort to keep his mind on the conversation. "What were you thinking about?"

She shrugged, picking restlessly at the dress that covered her knees. It was slightly damp because it had absorbed some of the moisture from his dip in the pool. "I was thinking about the things I've remembered." Abruptly, her eyes filled with tears and she turned away from him. "My childhood was *good.* What happened?" The question was plaintive.

Kurt covered her hands with one of his, stilling the movement. "I don't know," he said softly, "but I promise you we'll find out."

She turned toward him again. "Thank you," she whispered. And to his astonishment, she leaned forward and pressed a kiss to his lips.

In retrospect, he realized it had been a chaste gesture of affection, but at the time, there was no way he could ignore her. Shock held him motionless for a long moment as her soft lips molded to his, then an instant roar of arousal shot through his system. *Just a touch,* he told himself. He had to hold her for a few moments, even if he couldn't do what he really wanted, which was strip her naked and keep her in bed for a week.

The hand resting on her back pulled her back against him, and he took control of the kiss, tilting her head back across his right arm. He turned her in his arms, angling her so that one of her breasts pushed against his chest, and when she gasped, he swept his tongue into her mouth, staking his claim.

He could feel the nipple of the breast pressing against him as hard as a small pebble, and he could feel his own arousal straining at the swim trunks he wore.

Gretchen's arms came up around his neck, and her hands speared through his dark hair, holding his head to her as he kept up the heated, drugging kisses. He slid his left hand from her knee slowly along her thigh, trailing it up over her hip to the curve of her slender waist. His fingers splayed wide, and he could feel her ribs beneath the thin fabric of the dress and her bathing suit. When she didn't object, he slowly, slowly, moved his hand up some more. Still kissing her, he cupped his palm beneath the sweet curve of one breast, delighting in the way she filled his hand. Her nipple beaded immediately and she made a small, muffled sound that he swallowed greedily. He whisked his thumb over her nipple and she whimpered again. Her mouth was twisting beneath his now, seeking and tasting and testing, and he delighted in her responsiveness.

He wanted to touch her, *needed* to touch her, and his hand drifted down again. Reaching for the hem of her dress, he gently put a hand on her bare knee. She startled a little at the touch, but relaxed almost instantly, and a sense of gratification rushed through him. Slowly he caressed her knee in small circles, gradually extending the circles up her thigh as he went. As Gretchen continued to respond to his kisses, he shifted her slightly on his lap, sliding her back so that her bottom pressed firmly against his erection just so he could torment himself.

He slid his mouth from hers then, tasting the sweet tender flesh along her jaw and the delicate length of her neck, then moving lower. With unerring instinct, he nuzzled at her breast for an instant before he found her nipple, hard as a little berry even through the thin fabric of her bathing suit and covering dress and he immediately clamped his mouth over her and began to suckle strongly.

She arched against him with a strangled cry. Unable to think, to stop himself, he moved his hand between her thighs, rubbing her moist center. Her legs instinctively pressed together, holding him tight, and he wished like hell that it was another part of his anatomy instead of his hand.

Then he realized that he was moving, rocking his hips against her steadily, and he had to grit his teeth as pleasure threatened to explode. Forcing himself to stillness, he released her and lifted his head.

He looked down at her. Her lips were swollen, her eyes heavy-lidded. In their lovely dark depths were distinct wonder and a deep pleasure that nearly succeeded in eradicating his good intentions.

"This has to stop," he said, and his voice was so hoarse and husky he was shocked.

Awareness invaded her gaze and she began to struggle off his lap. He easily subdued her, but her lashes lowered, hiding her eyes from him, and she turned her head away, withdrawing in the only way she could. "I'm sorry," she said in a muffled tone. "You were just being kind and I threw myself at you. I understand."

"You don't understand one single thing." He took her chin in his hand and turned her face back to his. "Look at me."

Slowly, she lifted her eyelashes. "I've never behaved like this before in my entire life," she informed him. "I barely know you."

"That's bullshit," he said roughly. "You've told me about your life, remember? I'm willing to bet you know me better than you know another living person on the planet."

It was true, and he could see it reflected in her eyes.

"I want to make love with you," he said, his tone low and savage. "But I'm not taking advantage of you when you're emotionally distressed and out of your element." Although it was a damn fine line he was walking. A big part of him was questioning his sanity.

She studied his face some more. After a moment she stretched up and kissed his lips lightly. Probably as she had originally intended to, he thought, wanting to kick himself. "Thank you," she said.

"I'm going now." He shifted her away from him reluctantly and stood. "I'll see you at dinner."

It was a damn good thing his own room was just four down from hers, he thought as he entered it. Right now what he wanted was a cold shower.

That wasn't exactly what he wanted, he thought as he eased his swim trunks off and turned on the water. He wanted Gretchen naked and straining beneath him, wanted to be buried as deeply in her as he could get, wanted to feel her delicate internal shivering as he made her come around him.

But he was pretty sure that simply having sex with her wasn't going to help him stop thinking about her every waking minute.

When had that occurred, he wondered as he stood beneath the stinging spray of the shower. She was a job. Just a job.

Right. Gretchen was no "just" anything. She fascinated him, interested him sexually and intellectually. It had been years since he'd let himself get so hooked on a woman—eight years, to be exact. Since Karey. She'd been a cop, too. They'd been planning their wedding when he'd been involved in the shootout in which his partner had been killed.

And when she'd realized that sticking with him might tarnish her career, she hadn't been able to rip the ring off her finger fast enough.

Karey and Gretchen couldn't be less alike, he assured himself. Karey had known how to handle herself with men. She'd been beautiful and she'd known and accepted it as her due. She certainly hadn't been a deep thinker, and while she'd been perfectly correct on the job, she'd been a harmless flirt as well.

Gretchen, on the other hand, wouldn't know how to flirt if her life depended on it. She brought out his protective instincts in a way no other woman ever had—and that wasn't all. If he'd ever wanted Karey this badly, he couldn't remember it. Sex with her had been easy and fun and explosive. But he'd never felt the tenderness nor the bone-deep need he felt for Gretchen.

God, she was so innocent! He could tell from the tentative way she let him take the lead that she hadn't had a lot of experience with men. Then an ugly thought occurred to him. Would she respond like that to any patient, experienced man?

The mere thought made him want to snarl aloud. If he had anything to say about it, Gretchen wasn't going to get near another man. He wasn't sure how this was all going to shake out but he recognized that sooner or later he was going to have to address the feelings he was currently doing his best to ignore.

They met for breakfast in the hotel dining room the following morning. Afterward, he talked her into taking a day off, and they spent the day wandering through some of Cairo's smaller museums, mosques and Coptic churches. As they were walking around the sprawling Khan al-Khalili marketplace, she turned to him and said, "I remembered my father last night. It might be the same memory from the first time, because he walked down from the house to join us."

"What, exactly, do you remember?"

She actually smiled. "My father was a great big

bear of a man. He had dark hair and glasses. I remember him coming down the beach path and grabbing my mother from behind, kissing her. My brother Jay—I think that's his name—and the other two—'' She broke off, looking frustrated. ''I feel like their names are right there on the tip of my tongue, but I can't quite get them out.''

''You will.'' He squeezed her hand. ''What were your brothers doing?''

Gretchen began to speak again, but a part of Kurt's brain was assimilating and comparing information—and coming to some very disturbing conclusions. Oliver's iron-gray hair could once have been dark, but he was in no way a ''great, big bear.'' Kurt himself was six feet tall and Gamble was several inches shy of that, and thin, with a narrow frame.

''He'd built the most amazing sand toy,'' Gretchen continued. ''It was a sand-mover but it had special arms on it that could mold the sand once it was dropped where the boys wanted it. They built some pretty elaborate castles with the thing.'' A faint frown crossed her face.

''What is it?'' He was becoming so attuned to the nuances of her expression that he could tell something was disturbing her.

''I also had a dream last night, only it was more like a nightmare. I can't swear it's a memory but I think it might be.''

''Do you still recall it?''

She nodded. ''That's one reason I think it's a real

memory. Instead of fading and getting harder to remember, it's completely clear in my mind." She shuddered. "It sure would explain why I'm so afraid of both fire and water."

His eyebrows arched expectantly.

"I'm in the water when it begins." She took a deep breath, clearly agitated, and he took her hands in his. They were shaking and he realized how strongly this was affecting her. "There's a woman with me—maybe my mother—and we're both swimming. She's encouraging but I'm so tired. There's a small boat ahead of us that we're swimming toward." She paused, and he squeezed her hands encouragingly. "And then there's this huge, bright flash behind me. I look around and there's a boat—well, two halves of a boat—and they're burning, and then something slams into me and I go rolling through the water. I can't find the surface and I'm choking—and that's where it ends."

"Jesus." He was shaken. No wonder she had problems with fire and water. If this was truly something that had occurred when she was a child of twelve or even younger, she'd probably been completely traumatized. "It sounds like you were swimming away from a boat when it exploded," he thought aloud. "The shock wave from the blast might explain what you just described." And would more than account for her reluctance to go near water.

He called Gamble again from his own room while she showered and changed for dinner.

"I just need to check some details." Kurt reeled off some of the information Gamble had already shared with him, to which Gamble responded with a series of curt affirmatives. Then he said, "And you said she's an only child, right?" He'd been waiting to slip the query in unobtrusively.

"Why?" There was a sharp edge to the blunt demand. In Kurt's opinion, it was a damned strange reaction.

"Gretchen was really hoping she'd have some siblings somewhere," Kurt lied. God, it was surprisingly easy to fabricate a story. "She was an only child in her adopted home as well."

"She doesn't." The voice was flat and unemotional.

"All right. Just one more thing. Gretchen has a fear of water. She thinks she may have been involved in a boating accident at one time. Is that true?"

"A boating accident," Gamble repeated. He sounded completely blank, as if the words meant nothing. "No, I don't— Oh, wait a minute. When she was small we took her fishing with us one day and she fell overboard. I got her out right away, no harm done, but it may have resulted in the kind of fear you're describing." He paused. "So when are you bringing her to me?"

"When she's finished her research here. There isn't a timetable, is there?"

"No." Gamble's tone changed to a rather whiny lament. "It's just that we've been separated for so long and I've missed her so much. I'm afraid I'm very anxious to see her again."

Okay, now the bullshit meter was bouncing off the charts. It had hopped into overdrive when Gamble had spouted that lame story about falling into the water. A story that didn't address the explosion she'd described. "I'm sure she's just as eager to meet you." Kurt was mildly appalled at how easily the second lie came out. He couldn't stand liars and cheats, had little regard for anyone who behaved dishonorably. He didn't have any proof that Gamble was any of those things, but he couldn't convince himself that he was wrong to be suspicious of his client.

Until now his outlook on life had been as black-and-white as they came. Either you were ethical or you weren't. Either you were wrong or you were right. Either you were truthful or you were a liar. For the first time he saw that there might be times when there were shades of gray. And he couldn't shake the feeling that his lies were necessary to protect Gretchen.

In another test for Gamble, he said, "Can you tell me any more about her early life? She's very curious."

"Oh, no, that wouldn't be wise," Gamble said immediately. "I did consult the psychologist I mentioned and he believes that trying to jog her memory by supplying her with verbal perceptions would be unwise and possibly dangerous to her mental health.

In fact, he would like to be involved in her care when she comes home.''

Kurt didn't like the sound of that. Not at all. ''Don't you think you're jumping the gun a little bit? Maybe Gretchen doesn't want to see a shrink.''

''That is none of your concern, Miller. You were hired to find the girl and bring her to us. Nothing more, nothing less. So I'd suggest that if you want to see the rest of your overinflated fee, you do your job. Soon.''

Find the girl and bring her to us. The sharp words carried an ominous ring. Under any other circumstances, Kurt would be kicking himself for letting his imagination run away with him. But the sensation of evil—that was the only word for it, that emanated from Gamble's angry voice only fueled his concern.

Then a single word leaped out of the conversation at him. *Bring her to* us. *To* us. Just who in hell was ''us''?

Nine

"Hello?"

"Croft?"

"I've told you not to use last names over the phone!"

"Sorry." Oliver Grimble said in a placating tone. "Agnes and I suspect we might have a problem in Egypt."

"What kind of problem?"

"The investigator we hired to make contact with Grace—ah, Gretchen—seems reluctant to press her to meet us. Me."

"What has he done?"

"Nothing, really. He asks for a lot of information to share with her. Of course, I'm giving him nothing," Grimble said hastily. "He says she has two more weeks of work before she'll leave Cairo and that she'll consider a meeting then."

"*Two weeks?* Did he tell her the story about being in line to inherit a fortune?"

"Ah, she wasn't interested in money."

"Two weeks," Willard Croft said again. "I'd

hoped to have her reprogrammed and in place by then. We may need her to get to some of the others.''

"Two weeks may be the best we can hope for,'' Grimble said nervously.

''Is there anything else?''

''Well, we aren't sure, but we're afraid this investigator may be questioning the biological-parent story. He's been asking increasingly pointed questions.''

Croft grunted. ''Do what you can to back him off. If the girl won't come to us willingly, we'll have to consider other methods.''

''Let's write down everything you remember. Start with people.''

Kurt and Gretchen were seated in a quiet corner of the lobby bar, where he'd met her after she finished work that day. They'd talked casually over sandwiches, but now she could tell he wanted to discuss serious matters.

''All right.'' She took a deep breath. ''My mother and father.'' She repeated the descriptions she'd given him before. ''Three brothers, one sister. One of the brothers is named Jay.'' She stopped, something nagging at the corners of her mind. ''Or maybe his name just starts with *J*. The more I think about it, something doesn't seem quite right.''

''All right. Anyone else?''

She hesitated. ''No one I can clearly recall. Every once in a while I have an impression of a couple of other people who might have lived with us. Or near us. Friends of my parents, perhaps, but I can't put names or faces to them."

"Yet," he said.

She nodded, hoping he was right.

"Okay. Now places."

"The beach," she said promptly. "I think we must have spent a lot of time there."

"If your home was right on the beach, that would make sense."

"And then," she said, "there's that incident in the water. I've been running that through my head, and several things occur to me."

"Such as?" he nodded encouragingly.

"I think it was daylight. When I looked back at the explosion, I can see it pictured against a clear blue sky."

Kurt was writing as she spoke.

"Also, I don't remember extreme cold, so the water must have been temperate. Perhaps it was summer?"

"Or you were far enough south that the waters are always warm."

She shot him a skeptical look. "I don't think so. If we lived where it was warm all the time, we wouldn't have needed coats, would we?"

"You remember wearing a coat?"

She hesitated. "I don't have a specific memory of cold weather in which I needed a coat, or of putting on one. But I can picture a red jacket with a hood that…feels like it was mine.'' She sighed. ''I guess that doesn't help, does it?''

Kurt shrugged. ''I'm inclined to believe that you should trust your instincts.'' He set aside the pad and pencil and rose, coming around to offer his hand as she also rose. ''I think we should call it an early night. You seem tired.''

Grateful, she let him lead her toward the elevator. ''I haven't been sleeping well at all the past few nights. I wake up thinking that I was dreaming about my family, but I can't recall anything.''

Kurt had his arm draped loosely about her shoulders, holding her close to his warm, muscled body. ''I thought you seemed tense.''

'''Tense' is a mild word for what I'm feeling,'' she agreed. ''Now that I've begun to remember my family, I want to get this all resolved. As soon as I'm finished here, I want you to take me to meet my father.'' Then she frowned, renewed frustration in her slender body. ''If he even is my father.''

''Why would you say that?'' He sounded startled.

She lifted a hand. ''I don't know. I keep saying it just doesn't feel right but that's the only way to describe it.'' She laughed, but there was little humor in the sound. ''There I go again.''

Kurt took her key card from her hand and opened the electronic lock on her door. He ushered her forward so the door wouldn't close again. ''As I said, don't discount your feelings.'' He hesitated, then said, ''I'll call a friend of mine tomorrow and ask him to investigate Gamble. I tried once before but my friend must have been out of town.''

She turned and looked up at him, struck by the sense that he was trying to tell her something without coming right out and saying it.

Kurt hadn't been anticipating her stop, and he bumped into her. His big body felt as solid as concrete against her much softer one, and she suddenly couldn't take a deep enough breath, as if being so close to him sucked all the oxygen right out of the atmosphere. He grabbed her waist at the same time as she grasped his biceps to steady herself.

Her gaze was snared in his. His eyes became black fire as his gaze dropped to her mouth. She lifted herself on tiptoe, sliding her arms about his neck, shivering as his stirring erection filled the tender hollow in the cleft of her thighs.

A wave of tenderness, of need, of *love,* washed through her. How she needed him! In just days he'd become the center of her world, and she knew with certainty that her heart was his.

''Kurt,'' she whispered.

He closed his eyes, groaned. She saw his Adam's apple move as he swallowed. His hands tightened on her waist so hard that she felt his fingers bite in. For an instant, she thought he was going to lower his head—

And then he thrust her away from him.

''No,'' he said. ''I can't kiss you again.''

She was stunned, too shocked to be hurt. "Why not?"

"I— You're a job," he said. "It would be unethical."

She relaxed. "I won't be a part of your investigation much longer," she said. "As soon as you deliver me to my father, your obligation ends."

But still he shook his head. "Gretchen," he said, "you know I want you. But...this wouldn't be right." He gestured with agitation to the bed beyond them. "You deserve someone who can give you more than I can."

She shook her head, setting her mouth in a stubborn line. "Wrong. You have exactly what I want." She'd intended it to sound teasing, to reassure him, but it came out sounding strangely intense.

In any case, he was already releasing her waist, stepping back and removing her hands from around his neck. "No," he said. "You're about as vulnerable as they come right now. I'll support you but not like this."

And before she could respond, he turned and strode out of the room, letting the heavy door slam behind him.

She stood, openmouthed, where he'd left her. She didn't know whether to cuss or chase him and kiss him. He'd said something similar before but she'd had no idea he was so serious about it.

Her body felt strange and sensitive, achy with the need to be next to his. Her one sexual experience had been nothing more than a dry exercise in copulation, nothing like the overwhelming experience she'd read about in books and magazines. Somehow, she had a feeling that with Kurt, there'd be nothing dry or clinical about making love.

His consideration warmed her and confirmed what she'd been afraid to even let herself think until today: Kurt was coming to care for her.

She hugged herself, repressing the urge to dance around the room. She wasn't quite sure when she'd first begun to love him, but she figured it had been within hours of their first meeting. And if he loved her, too… The future suddenly looked much rosier than it ever had before. She couldn't resist thinking of marriage. And along with marriage came children.

Happiness so overwhelming she felt as if she would explode welled up within her. Children! Someone biologically related to her *and* someone whose very cells would link Kurt and her forever.

She hadn't given her recent resolve to have a child of her own a single thought in the days since she'd met Kurt. All her thoughts had been about him. And now… Now it looked as though she might have a chance at a normal life like other women, a life she'd never expected she would know. A life she'd been determined would include a child one way or another. This way was definitely best.

Now all she had to do was make him admit that they belonged together. He thought she was vulnerable and confused, and that he was doing the right thing. But she couldn't feel any less confused about this, she was sure.

And she'd just have to make him believe it, too.

That evening he arrived punctually to take her to dinner. Gretchen had worked late on purpose. She had A Plan. Kurt wanted to make love to her, she was certain. All he needed was a little push. And once he did, he'd see how right they were for each other.

"Just a minute," she called. She had taken a leisurely shower and had just wrapped herself in a thick bathrobe provided by the hotel. She'd timed this down to the minute, knowing how punctual he was.

When she opened the door, Kurt's eyebrows rose. "I'm not sure they'll let you in a restaurant in that attire." He shrugged, smiling.

"I worked late," she said. Perfectly true. "I'll be ready in a minute." She took his hand and tugged, and to her relief he let her lead him into the room.

"Take your time." He crossed to the window, folding his arms over his chest.

"Have you seen this month's article that *National Geographic* did about the Ahk Tablets?" she asked.

He nodded. "Your father read it—that's what made him think you might be his daughter. He showed it to me."

She picked up the magazine and went to him, flipping through the pages until she found the article. "They did a nice job explaining the project." She held the magazine up at breast level so that he would have to look down at it—and down at the place where the robe met over her bare skin, revealing the upper swells of her breasts.

Kurt's eyelids veiled his thoughts, but he suddenly was still. Not still so much as suspended, she decided. He didn't even take a breath for the longest time. Heady female satisfaction rushed through her as she sensed the struggle going on inside him.

"Kurt—"

"Go get dressed." His voice was hoarse. He took the magazine from her and turned his back to her abruptly.

Gretchen took a deep breath. She'd embarked upon this course, now all she had to do was find the courage to pursue it. She'd hoped he would make it a little easier. Slowly, she pulled the tie of the robe free. The fabric parted down the front.

"Kurt?" She took a deep breath and reached for resolve.

He turned back around. "What?" he barked. Then he froze, his gaze riveted to the pale line of skin that peeped from beneath the open robe, the shadow of cleavage visible, the little indentation of her navel. His eyes lingered at the vee of her thighs, where crisp black curls sheltered her most feminine flesh. She knew what he was seeing. She'd practiced in front of the mirror, trying to work up her nerve.

"What the hell are you doing?" His voice was hoarse.

"What does it look like?" She shrugged delicately, letting the robe slide off her shoulders to pool around her feet. She was breathing so fast she was afraid she might hyperventilate, but she forced herself not to grab for the robe and cover herself as she longed to do.

The magazine hit the floor. His fingers actually flexed. "It looks—" he licked his lips "—damned good. But, Gretchen—"

"Kurt." She stepped forward, linking her arms around his neck and pressing her bare flesh against him. She felt horribly embarrassed and exposed, her skin tender and unbearably sensitive against his fully clothed body. If he rejected her now, she'd probably just go off somewhere and die of shame. "Please," she whispered into his neck. "Make love to me."

There was a frozen instant when she sensed that he intended to refuse. But then his hands came up, gliding from her smooth, silky bottom to her shoulders and back down again. He cupped her buttocks, slowly kneading them as if he couldn't help himself, and a dark, intense fire lit his eyes. "I didn't want to do this," he said in a low, rough voice, "but I'll be damned if I can walk away from you now."

He bent his head to her shoulder, setting his teeth in her sensitive skin and nipping lightly. She squeaked, unprepared for the small, stinging pain, but then he laved the spot with his tongue, taking away the pain and replacing it with a taut, expectant pleasure.

She pressed herself more tightly against him until he bent and put an arm beneath her knees, lifting her into his arms as if she weighed nothing. "Mine," he said, carrying her to the bed in three long strides. He lay her down and stepped back, stripping off his shirt, socks, shoes and pants without ever removing his gaze from her body.

Beneath the pants he wore plain white briefs. He was already so aroused that his sex was barely contained, and he winced as he carefully pulled the elastic band down and quickly shucked the briefs off as well.

Then he was naked, and Gretchen had her first doubts about the wisdom of her plan. Kurt was a big man, his shoulders broad, his arms roped with sinew. Plates of muscle rippled across his chest and abdomen, and a thick dark pelt of silky hair matted his breastbone. The hair arrowed down in a bold line to his groin.

Panic seized her as she stared at the evidence of his desire for her. Before she could scramble off the bed and explain that this had been a mistake, he put a knee on the mattress and lowered himself to her, coming down half atop her. She moaned, excited and aroused despite her fears, when the hard ridge pressed firmly against her hip. He gathered both her arms above her head, anchoring them with one big fist, and bent a knee over hers to hold her in place.

"Baby, you're beautiful." He cupped a breast, plumping it into a full, round globe, and then he bent his head and took one nipple into his mouth, swirling his tongue around it. Gretchen squirmed as lightning streaks of wild sensation rushed from her breast to her belly, leaving her quivering with need. She tugged futilely at her arms but he didn't release her.

"Lie still," he said. "Let me love you."

The words reassured her as nothing else could have, and she did relax. His free hand circled her throat, then trailed down between her breasts and moved on to explore the gentle dip of her navel. He circled it three times, then let a single finger slide down her belly, and by then she was so sensitive to his slightest touch that she arched off the bed with a gasp. He splayed his big hand flat over her abdomen, rubbing in small circles until she didn't think she could stand it anymore and she rotated her hips wildly, asking wordlessly for something more.

He moved over her then, settling himself heavily between her thighs, and she felt his erection prodding at her.

She opened her mouth but he kissed her then, his tongue taking advantage, seeking out hers and coaxing her into exploring the heated interior of his mouth as thoroughly as he had hers.

He put a hand between them and she felt his finger slipping down between her legs, rubbing lightly over her soft folds and probing gently when they parted for him. She was completely unprepared, though, when he pushed one finger deep into her, and she cried out beneath his mouth.

"Easy, baby," he said in a hoarse, deep voice she barely recognized. "Easy." His finger worked in and out of her and she could feel herself softening, moistening, clinging around his finger as a fine wire of tension drew taut deep in her abdomen. Then he withdrew his finger and she felt his sex in its place, steadily exerting pressure against her tender opening. He slipped in a little way and stopped.

She opened her eyes and looked up at him. His face was drawn and tense. "You're so tight," he said through gritted teeth. "It feels so good."

He wasn't hurting her, she realized, slightly surprised. She felt an urgency to move, and without really thinking about it, she rocked her hips beneath him, admitting even more of his hard shaft. He was so big she felt stretched beyond measure, and yet there was no pain.

Her one uncomfortable experience the night she'd lost her virginity had never affected her like this. The sex had taken place on a couch in the dark, and his hands had been rough and eager. He hadn't taken the time to arouse her as Kurt had, and she'd been dry and so tight he'd hurt her when he'd shoved his way into her. This time was different. In more ways than one.

Kurt was still slowly pushing forward. He pulled her knees up, spreading them wider and she felt him settle even deeper. "That's it," he said in a dark, husky voice. "Take it all." He dropped his head and found her breast, his mouth clamping hard over her nipple as he began to suckle strongly. The immediate connection between her breast and her womb made her cry out sharply and arch against him, and he muttered, "Yeah, that's it," as his hips began to withdraw.

"No." She protested instinctively, setting her hands on his lean buttocks and trying to hold him in place.

He chuckled deep in his throat, then surged heavily forward again. "Is this what you want?"

She couldn't speak, could only gasp as his motion pushed him hard against the sensitive little nub at the top of her opening. A shock wave rippled through her and she saw on his face that he'd felt it, too.

"You're going to make me come doing that," he warned her. And then he began to move again, his hand slipping beneath her to palm her bottom and hold her in place as he pounded against her, moving in and out faster and faster until she was crying out with each thrust and pushing her hips up to meet him.

It was too much, too much pleasure. The fist that had clenched so tightly inside her suddenly flew apart and she exploded beneath him, waves of rhythmic muscle contractions dragging her hard against him over and over.

His slick, iron-hard body went rigid against her, and she could feel his hips jerking as he pumped himself into her in repeated bursts of warm, wet release. She was so sensitive that every time he moved, he sent another small shock wave rushing through her, and it wasn't until he finally collapsed on her in a heavy, delightfully masculine heap that she was able to relax and savor the astonishing glow of the satisfaction he'd given her.

Kurt was biting his tongue. Literally. He had the damnedest urge to blurt out completely insane things to Gretchen as they lay together in pleasant drowsiness, and the need to speak was ruining the sweetness of the moment for him.

She was becoming too important to him. He'd sworn he would never let another woman matter too much.

But how much was too much? As much as Gretchen was beginning to matter, he was afraid.

Part of him wanted to get the hell out of there.

But he couldn't force himself to move. He'd rolled to his back when they'd finally found the strength to move, pulling her into his arms. She'd settled herself against him so naturally, so perfectly that he was a little shocked. He'd never felt quite this way before, not even with Karey, whom he'd thought he loved.

And that was why he wanted to run. He wanted to *talk,* for God's sake. What sane man wanted to talk after having sex? But there were questions burning in his mind that he wanted—*needed*—answered, and so he opened his mouth and voiced the thought that had been burning in his brain. "Were you a virgin?"

She was idly brushing the thick hair that matted over his breastbone. "No," she said quietly. "But in terms of pleasure, I was definitely a novice.'' She lifted her head, her eyes worried. ''Did I do something wrong?''

He almost laughed aloud, but she was serious, and he didn't want to hurt her feelings. ''Professor, if you did things any more *right,* I might have died right here in your arms.'' He snorted. ''No, baby, you didn't do anything wrong. I just wondered...'' He hesitated. ''You seemed a little...new to this. And you were so tight I was afraid I was hurting you.''

He wasn't certain but he thought she blushed. ''You didn't hurt me,'' she said with certainty. ''I had no idea making love could be so...perfect.''

It *had* been damn near perfect. But the way she'd said ''making love'' made him nervous. Didn't she realize this was just a normal, healthy encounter between two consenting adults?

And he had another concern. ''So you're not using birth control?'' he asked, though he feared he already knew the answer.

Her body tensed but then he felt her relax. ''You don't have to worry about conception,'' she said. ''I'm not a girl who leaves things to chance.''

He felt relief wash over him. And selfish pleasure—the last thing he wanted was the barrier of a condom between them.

''I only ever did this with one other man,'' she said, distracting him. ''He was one of my professors.''

He thought about that for a moment, thoroughly

disliking the thought of her with anyone else. "Older than you, I take it?" God, he hoped the guy had known what he was doing.

"Yes. A lot."

Her jerky delivery made his heart sink. He had a feeling he wasn't going to like what he was about to hear.

"I was young. And incredibly stupid."

"Naive, maybe," he said gently. "But stupid? I don't think so."

The corners of her lips lifted a little, but he knew it was because she thought he expected her to smile.

"It wasn't much fun."

He could have laughed at her understatement, but there was nothing funny about the thought of Gretchen being carelessly seduced and dumped by some college teacher out to add a few more student notches to his bedpost. "I'm sure it wasn't," he said, keeping the anger he felt out of his tone. "What happened?"

The smile died and her lips trembled. "Looking back, I realize I was flattered at the attention. No one had ever shown any interest in me before. And my parents hadn't been dead very long, so I was lonely, too. We had a few research meetings at his house that he called dates and one night he took me to bed."

Kurt tightened his arms around her, pulling her more closely to his chest and rubbing his hand up and down her back, silently trying to soothe the hurt that colored her voice.

"It was nothing like this!" The mild astonishment in her voice surprised a chuckle out of him.

"I certainly hope not," he said with feeling. He rolled, holding her to him so that she was beneath him, and settled himself between her thighs, sighing in contentment as his hips found the sweet, warm spot where her legs parted. He was getting hard again, and he gently probed her soft little opening until he had worked himself inside her, capturing the small sounds she made with his mouth. He thrust gently a few times and when he was deeply snuggled in the tight channel, he sighed with pleasure. "I could sleep here just like this."

Then he felt her hips rock subtly beneath him, her soft, moist flesh sliding back and forth over his shaft and he swore as arousal flexed his hips involuntarily within her. "On second thought," he said, "who needs sleep?"

A long time later, he found the strength to raise his head from where he'd buried it in the pillow beside hers. His hands found hers, and he laced his fingers with hers, holding her palms out on either side of her head as he looked down at her. "Thank you," he said softly. "Thank you for trusting me to make this good for you."

Her eyes were wide and solemn as she gazed up at him. Then she smiled, warm happiness reflected in the blue depths of her marvelous eyes. "I should be thanking you. You showed me what making love should be like.''

There it was again. That phrase. ''Making love.'' The term was a mere euphemism. He'd used it himself without meaning in it its most basic context. It was rarely taken literally and he doubted Gretchen even realized what she had said.

Beneath him she suddenly yawned. A red tide of color rose in her cheeks. ''I'm sorry,'' she said. ''It's not the company, honest.''

He grinned, relieved to be off the subject of love. ''It's late.'' He released her hands and rolled to his back, drawing her against his side. ''We could both use the sleep.''

Gretchen didn't protest, merely cuddled against him, one hand splayed flat on his chest. He was pleased that she didn't question his intent to sleep right there with her curled against him.

Ten

Jake Ingram woke with a start. The dream had been so vivid that for a moment he was completely disoriented. Then the familiar night-shadowed outlines of the furniture in his bedroom began to swim into dim view as he stared into the dark, his heart pounding.

Damn. He wondered if there was a way to get at the memories hiding beneath the surface of the new life he'd assumed when his mother had spirited his siblings and him away from danger when they were children.

There had to be. He refused to live the rest of his life like this, with tantalizing glimpses of his past sneaking up to haunt him when he least expected them.

He took deep breaths, forcing himself to relax as he brought the remnants of the dream to mind. He'd been on a beach. He was certain it was the beach in North Carolina where they'd lived in his father's family home, according to Vi—according to his mother.

He wasn't sure he would ever be able to call Vi

that. In his mind, his mother would always be the only woman whom he could recall raising him—Zach's mother. Not his, not really. No, his mother was a surprisingly pretty dark-haired woman with a scar on her forehead.

And even though he barely knew her, he got a funny, tight feeling in his throat when he thought about what she'd gone through to save the lives of her children.

Now it was his responsibility to save them from the newest threat his parents' old enemies represented.

He wished he could remember more about his siblings. Right now, all he had were these damned dreams and fuzzy images that plagued him. Like the dream he'd just had.

He'd been on the beach with a girl, building an elaborate sandcastle. In fact, he had a distinctly amusing memory of a younger, smaller boy—had that been Gideon?—pouring a bucket of seawater over his sister's head.

The amusement faded as he recalled what the media was saying now about the boy once known as Gideon. *Who is Achilles?* That headline, in particular, often replayed itself in his mind. He knew exactly who Achilles was, if Violet was correct. And she was, he was certain of it. Jake might not remember much, but what he did recall jived exactly with the fantastic story she had shared with him in D.C. *President Demands Swift Justice,* another remembered headline blared. Was there any way to save Gideon? Jake had to assume his brother didn't remember who he really was. Violet's frightening story about the brainwashing and implanted memories had him worried. Was there any way to reach Gideon?

The elements of the dream returned and he felt himself consciously relax as he let the memory of the love and warmth in that moment wash over him. His other siblings had been on the beach that day as well as his parents. His mother sat on a blanket in the sand with the smaller girl in her lap, engrossed in storytelling, while the other littler boy jumped waves holding on to his dad's big, capable hands.

Abruptly, the peaceful quality shattered when his mother looked up and frowned. He turned to see what was wrong. Two people were coming down to the beach, and he got a strong feeling of...*revulsion* was the only word for it. What the hell?

His father came out of the water despite the little kids' protests and took up a position right behind his mother, arms crossed and feet planted. The position was clearly one of challenge, and Jake was sure, without quite knowing how, that he wouldn't want to be on the receiving end of the big man's displeasure.

The people drew nearer and as their faces came into view, Jake felt another shock, another seismic shift of present-day and the past as they realigned themselves to fit together. He knew those people! Not just in his memory, but in the present. He'd met them at the Bluebonnet Ball when they'd horned in on a conversation he was having with David Castlemane.

Agnes Payne and Oliver Gamble. But that wasn't right, was it? Violet had told him it wasn't Gamble, it was Grimble.

He'd known the pair as Aunt Agnes and Uncle Ollie when he was growing up. They'd tried to get him to stay overnight at their home not far from Jake's own on several occasions but he and his sister had always managed to wriggle out of it. They'd taken the younger set of triplets, though, he recalled. God knew what the pair had been up to when they'd had the smaller children. Jake hadn't liked Aunt Agnes or Uncle Ollie one little bit, and though he couldn't remember why, he suspected it was a child's intuitive distrust of people whom he sensed didn't really care for children.

Again, he realized that Violet had been right. At the ball, those two must have been trying to plan how to snatch him—but they'd later taken Zach instead. His blood ran cold at the thought of what could have happened to his adoptive brother, and he thanked God for Maisy, now Zach's wife, who had realized the pair were up to no good and helped Zach escape.

With a renewed sense of urgency, he realized he had to contact his sister Gretchen right away. When he'd called Harvard, he'd been told she was on a sabbatical in London. So he'd called the University College London, only to learn she was still on the Egyptian project in Cairo. She'd been expected back within the month and he'd planned to contact her then. But now he realized he couldn't wait. She might not remember anything of her past and probably would think he was crazier than a bedbug, but if the pair and their cronies had figured out Jake's real identity, it was a safe bet that someone as visible in the scientific community as Gretchen Wagner had come to their notice as well.

As he began to try to relax enough to get back to sleep, he promised himself that tomorrow he'd begin trying to get in touch with his sister.

Early morning's bright light began to play around the edges of the heavy curtains that protected the windows of Gretchen's bedroom at the Nile Hilton.

Kurt woke slowly. He knew instantly that Gretchen's head was the weight on his right arm, her hair the fragrant silky warmth against which his cheek rested. He also realized his morning erection was rock-hard and clearly expecting some action, snuggled as it was into the sweet crease of her bottom.

Without really thinking about it, he shifted his hips slightly, nudging insistently at her. The sensation was exquisite, and he reached down with his left hand, finding the soft curve of her hip. His fingers slid around her thigh, urging her leg up over his and exposing the velvety feminine core of her to his questing fingers. She was slick and so hot she practically sizzled at his touch, and with a sigh of sheer relief, he pushed himself forward, finding and opening her, steadily encroaching until his aching shaft was firmly lodged deep within her snug, wet channel.

Gretchen made a little mewing sound, and he swept his hand up her body to cup one breast in his big palm, finding the tender nipple and brushing his palm back and forth until it beaded into the tight little button that he loved.

''Good morning, Professor,'' he growled into her ear.

''Is this how they say it where you're from?'' Her voice was husky and aroused and full of laughter.

''That's how *I* say it when I've lost the battle for good intentions,'' he said. He slid his hand back down her body, splaying it flat against her belly as he began to thrust from behind her, holding her firmly against him.

She writhed on his impaling shaft, her body clenching around him like a glove. He felt his self-control waver dangerously. Sliding his hand down, he slipped one finger through her triangular patch of curls, finding and exposing the slippery little nub at the top of her cleft.

Gretchen made a short, strangled sound deep in her throat when his finger rubbed intimately over her. With no warning, she exploded around him. Her body bucked and trembled, her inner muscles squeezing him relentlessly as she came hard and fast, and that was all it took to send him over the edge. His hips pounded against her bottom, plunging out of control until he shuddered and arched heavily against her, half-pushing her into the mattress as he spilled his seed deep inside her in great, pulsing spasms.

Had it ever been this good before? he thought hazily as he struggled to regain his breath. He knew he must be crushing her but damned if he could move to save his life.

Finally, a measure of strength returned and he pushed himself backward off her, sliding out of her as he rolled to lie on his back. "Wow," he managed. "You're dangerous, woman."

"Only to you." She shifted onto her side to cuddle against him, and he turned his head and pressed a kiss against her temple.

They lay quietly for a while and he dozed, coming awake when she finally began to slide from the bed. "Where are you going?"

She gave him a wry look. "Bathroom. Unlike you, I don't have an infinite bladder capacity."

"It's a guy thing," he told her smugly.

The smile she shot him over her shoulder before she closed the bathroom door was enough to stir his pulse. "You're definitely all guy," she said.

Well, if that didn't make him feel like a king, what would? He heaved himself out of bed and stretched mightily, then snagged his clothes and began to step into his pants. He'd go back to his room and shower, then he guessed he'd kill another day somewhere while she wrapped up her research.

And then it would be night again. His heart beat

faster at the thought of spending another night with her snuggled in his arms, her silky skin his to touch, to taste any time he pleased.

He should be irritated that she'd sneaked beneath his guard and seduced him, but he couldn't. He'd wanted her desperately. And she'd wanted him just as much, so they'd acted on it. Serious attraction, intense sex. It was that simple.

His reasons for staying away from her didn't seem all that important now, and he couldn't remember why he'd been so adamant about it. He'd mostly been worried about her, worried that he was rushing her. A quick grin lit his hard features for a moment. They'd rushed, all right. Cairo would always have a special place in his memories.

Cairo. His satisfaction faded as he thought of leaving. With the exception of the night just past, he was beginning to be sorry he'd let her talk him into these two extra weeks. Some sixth sense was nagging at him, warning him to get Gretchen's meeting with the man who claimed to be her father over and done with.

But then Kurt's place in her life would be unnecessary. He would have no reason to keep seeing her.

He didn't even like thinking about it, especially now. Dammit, he wasn't ready to let her go yet.

So don't. The little voice made him pause. *You're not tied to Texas. Move to Boston. You can work there and still see her. And when it's over, then you can decide where you want to go next.* He considered the notion. Not a bad plan.

He was confident that, given enough time and proximity, he'd eventually get tired of Gretchen and she him, even if he couldn't imagine ever not wanting her the way he wanted her now. He'd promised himself eight years ago that he was finished with commitments. Relationships—real relationships based on something other than terrific sex—took work and honesty and trust. And he wasn't about to let a woman get under his skin and then rip his heart out ever again.

Gretchen came out of the bathroom moments later and looked surprised to see him dressed. "Leaving so soon?" Her voice sounded teasing but he could see a hint of hurt in her eyes.

He smiled and opened his arms, enjoying the swell of pleasure that accompanied her headlong rush into his embrace. She twined her arms around his neck and lifted her face for his kiss, then lay her head against his shoulder. "I love you," she murmured.

The words came at him with the force of a tidal wave, swamping his carefully arranged plans. "No, you don't," he said without stopping to think. He felt her body stiffen in his arms and he rushed to explain. "We have an incredible mutual physical attraction, but it's not love."

There was a moment of silence in the room. Gretchen didn't move. "Are you telling me how I feel?" Her voice was expressionless.

''No,'' he began, ''I just was—''

''—telling me how *you* feel,'' she said.

She hadn't moved away from him but he suddenly felt that she was on the other side of an enormous wall that couldn't be scaled. ''Uh, not exactly.''

She did move then, stepping back out of reach, and he saw that her face had lost the warm glow it had held after their early-morning lovemaking. ''I'm thirty-five years old,'' she said quietly, ''and I've never been in love, *really* in love, in my entire life. Until now. So if you don't feel the same way, I'd appreciate it if you'd just say so.''

Now he knew how it felt to be tossed into the sea when you couldn't swim. Panic seized him. ''I don't do love,'' he told her. ''Love doesn't exist. All you're feeling right now is what I'm feeling.''

''Which is?''

''Sexual attraction.'' He was sure of that. Wasn't he? ''And we have a lot in common.''

''Such as?''

He floundered. ''Well...''

''You're from Texas, I'm from the East Coast. Your background is law enforcement, mine is academia—''

''Neither of us has living family,'' he said, determined to show her. ''We both like to dance.''

''We have nothing of consequence in common, Kurt.'' Her voice was still quiet, but there was a chill in it deep enough to nip. ''What we *had*—what I thought we had—was the beginning of something that might have lasted for a lifetime.'' She stepped past him to the door and twisted the knob in one quick, efficient move, her eyes shadowed with a pain he'd caused. Holding the door wide, she made a sweeping gesture. ''Goodbye.''

If he thought he'd known panic before, he'd been truly mistaken. ''Gretchen, you're making more of this than it has to be. I like you. A lot. And last night...'' His voice dropped. ''Last night was like nothing I've ever experienced before. I want to be with you. It's just— You have to understand,'' he said desperately, ''I'm not looking for anything lasting.''

But she wasn't looking at him. Her gaze was fixed on the floor, and he could see that her hands were shaking where she held the doorknob. As he watched, a fat tear escaped and rolled down her cheek.

Something inside him tore wide open. He started across the room, reaching for her. ''Baby, please—''

But she stepped back again, out of reach. She reached up and swiped away the tear. ''On the other hand,'' she said steadily, ''I *am* looking for something lasting.'' Her gaze met his again and her blue eyes were flat and steady, as unreadable as her tone. If she still hurt, she'd hidden it well.

Unease trickled through him, though she hadn't really said anything unexpected. ''Like what?'' he asked warily, though he was sure he already knew the answer. Love. Commitment. Things in which he no longer believed.

"A baby," she said.

He was so startled that he didn't react for a minute. Finally, he said, "What?" He couldn't have heard her right.

She smiled then, but there was no warmth in it. "Like I said, I'm thirty-five years old. My biological clock has been ticking loudly for a long time. Just before we met, I decided I want a child." She inclined her head slightly. "So, in the event that you've accommodated my wish, thank you."

He shook his head. "Wait a minute. You can't just—"

"I won't ask you for money or anything else," she said soothingly. "After today you don't ever have to see me again so you won't even know if I got lucky."

"I'll be damned!" he roared. His head was spinning. Dammit. How could she do this? Had she been planning it all along?

He'd never considered having children. Karey and he had never even talked about it. Except for tonight, he'd always been careful to assume responsibility for protection. Tonight, he'd completely forgotten at first. And when he'd mentioned it, Gretchen had said—what *had* she said, exactly?

I'm not a girl who leaves things to chance.

Bitterly, he realized he'd been manipulated. And he couldn't even blame her completely. He'd helped. With no warning, a vivid memory assailed him: He was nine again, clinging to his grandmother's hand.

It was a stifling hot Texas summer day, and they were standing beneath a canopy in a cemetery while the preacher spoke over the caskets that contained all that was left of his parents after a car accident took their lives.

He knew they weren't coming back because he'd seen them before the funeral. They hadn't looked real anymore.

He was going to live with Grandmama. He didn't want to. He wanted Mama and Daddy to come home. He wanted Mama to pull him into her lap and hug and kiss him, even if he was too old for that mushy stuff anymore. He wanted her so bad he wouldn't even act like he hated her lovin' on him.

Why did they have to go to that party, anyway? It was just a dumb ol' grown-up thing, and Daddy had told Kurt he didn't really want to go, anyway.

Tears of anger rolled down his cheeks and splashed onto the hand his grandmama held. She looked down and pulled him hard against her, and he felt her belly shake. She was crying, too.

"Kurt?" Gretchen was looking at him curiously.

"No," he said hoarsely. Logically, he knew his parents hadn't wanted to leave him, hadn't abandoned him, but the angry little boy inside him protested that any child of his not suffer the same fate. "That's my baby, too."

She looked taken aback. "There's no reason to get upset about it. It's just a hypothetical baby at the moment."

"No reason to get upset? You use me for stud services and then tell me not to get upset?" He'd never wanted children, never wanted the responsibility for another little life. The very idea of some little person depending on him terrified him.

But it was too late for that. Deep inside him, he was abruptly certain that he'd made Gretchen pregnant last night. The thought scared him to death, but he was conscious of a startling feeling of relief as well. If she was pregnant, there would be no way she was ever getting rid of him.

"*I* used *you?*" Her tone was incredulous. "You just got done telling me all you felt was physical attraction, remember?"

He looked at her again, standing in the doorway with her arms crossed defiantly despite the telltale biting of her full lower lip that signaled nerves. "If you're pregnant," he said quietly, "I'll be stuck to you like gum on a hot sidewalk, baby."

Eleven

Gretchen tossed a pair of shoes into her open suitcase with an uncharacteristic lack of precision. She was still shocked by Kurt's reaction to what she'd said about a baby.

She'd only told him that she could be pregnant because he'd hurt her. In truth, she hadn't been thinking at all about contraception, or the lack of it, the night before. She felt her eyes filling with tears at the memory of his appalled expression when she'd told him she loved him. Why was she attracted to yet another man who could never love her? Maybe it was her. Maybe she just wasn't someone who could inspire love.

No. She rejected that pathetic notion. If she let another man destroy her self-worth again, it would be her own fault. She was *not* unlovable.

Quickly she packed the rest of her belongings haphazardly into her suitcases. She'd called the airline and taken care of her hotel bill; she was ready to leave Egypt. For some time she'd been fooling around with unnecessary but nice cleanup touches to the Ahk project while she considered the whole situation with Kurt's client. But in truth, she'd just been delaying meeting the man who said he was her father.

She should be thrilled. She should be ecstatic that at last there was someone who could provide the missing pieces of her early life. But she couldn't shake an entirely inappropriate feeling of apprehension and dread.

That was ridiculous. This man wasn't going to hurt her. He was her father. Maybe. Why was it she doubted that? And what reason would Mr. Gamble have for contacting her if he wasn't? She forced herself to dismiss her concerns. She would meet the man in person sometime in the next few days—she could deal with him then. She'd decided that once she was back in London, she would call Kurt's agency and ask him to set up a meeting. If she had Nancy make the call, she wouldn't even have to speak to Kurt, and she could request that he not attend the actual meeting with Mr. Gamble. There was no reason for him to do so, anyway.

The bellboy arrived and she bounced off the bed where she'd been sitting and opened the door. After instructing him on what she wanted done with her luggage, she went down to the lobby and caught a cab to the airport.

As she was driven through the streets of Cairo, hurt and sadness welled up and she had to dab at the tears that escaped. The past couple of weeks had been, without question, the most wonderful time of her life.

How could she have been so wrong about Kurt?

Granted, she didn't have much experience with men and she had to admit she was often a little out of the loop when it came to socializing, but she wasn't stupid. Intuition told her that there was something more—something that had nothing to do with her—behind Kurt's reaction to her declaration of love.

And his equally bizarre reaction to the thought of fathering a child. She hadn't really thought about it, but she supposed she'd assumed he wouldn't care.

She remembered again the shock on his face when she'd mentioned a child. And then it had been almost as if he'd forgotten she was there. Something he'd been thinking had disturbed him, she was sure. She wished she could ask him about it. But Kurt was still in Cairo and she was at the airport, the cabby opening her door before he hefted her suitcases out of his trunk. Besides, she reminded herself as the hurt and anger from earlier welled up, she was never speaking to him again.

Inside the terminal, she checked in and went directly to the international terminal where her flight was going out. She hadn't left herself a lot of time, and before she knew it, she was filing onto the plane and taking her seat.

She was just buckling her seat belt when Kurt lowered his big body into the empty seat beside her.

"Hello. I take it we're flying to London."

"I'm flying to London," she said when her heart had stopped trying to beat its way out of her chest. "I don't know what you're doing."

"I'm traveling with the mother of my child."

"If I'm pregnant, you have nothing to do with it," she said furiously.

"That's not the way I remember it." His voice was warm and silky with memories and she fell silent, her whole face burning. "You know," he said quietly, "fathers have a lot more rights than they used to. Especially if they want to be a part of their child's life."

She refused to discuss this with him anymore. She probably wasn't even pregnant, she thought resentfully. A pang squeezed her heart at the thought. What would it be like to have Kurt's baby? Her body was still tender in places from their prolonged lovemaking the night before, but someday all she would have would be memories. "How did you find me?" she asked dully.

"I'm beginning to understand the way your mind works," he informed her. "When things don't go your way, you pick up your toys and go home."

She was speechless for a moment. At last she said, "That's not a fair statement. You don't want me."

"That's not true and you know it." His voice was deep and caressing. "I just don't want to put labels on our relationship."

"What relationship? We had sex."

"We had *terrific* sex," he corrected, his eyes intent.

Abruptly she was furious again. "That's what you wanted, wasn't it?" she said. "And when you made it very clear that there was nothing *else* you wanted, I chose to move on. So go away and leave me alone.''

But he shook his head. ''Sorry, baby. That's the one thing I can guarantee you isn't going to happen.''

She fumed for the next five hours, sitting beside him in the tight confines of the airplane seats that pretty much ensured she couldn't avoid brushing against him from time to time. He figured she'd be a wealthy woman if she got a dollar for every evil glare she cast his way.

When they arrived at Heathrow, he followed her down to the baggage claim area and shouldered her two biggest bags before she could stop him. Short of making a scene right there—which he'd counted on Gretchen's quiet nature to prevent—there was nothing she could do but give him fulminating looks as he bundled her into a cab. She gave the address for her sub-leased flat, but Kurt overrode her and gave the cabbie the name of a hotel.

''You can't go back to your flat.'' He didn't care how much she argued, it wasn't happening. ''Until we find out why Gamble wants you so badly, I'd feel much better if you stayed close to me.''

She rolled her eyes. ''Your imagination is getting out of hand.''

He didn't have anything to say in response so he only looked at her.

''Oh, all right!'' she finally said. ''We'll do it your

way." And she flounced back into the far corner of the taxi without another word.

Evidently, she decided the only way to deal with him was to ignore him. Even when he followed her into the hotel and took a room as close to hers as he could manage, she didn't speak again. But as she was unlocking the door of her room, he stopped her with a hand on her arm.

"Gretchen."

She looked up at him, her eyes wounded and angry. "What?"

"I have to go out for a little while. When I get back, we need to talk."

"I have nothing to say to you."

"It's about my client. Your so-called father. He's flying to London today."

Her gaze sharpened. "You're going to meet with him, aren't you? Take me with you."

He shook his head. "I have a bad feeling about him. If I thought it was safe, you could go. But..." He shook his head. "I can't make you stay away, but I'm asking you to trust me on this."

"Trust you," she said slowly. But as she thought about it, she realized that while she might feel angry and hurt and humiliated by him, she *did* trust him. "I do trust you, Kurt," she said quietly.

She actually saw his body relax, his eyes warm, and he reached for her. But she read his intentions in his eyes, quickly stepping backward, one hand raised defensively. "I'm going to the university museum for a couple of hours. Call me when you get back."

He didn't place the call from the hotel because he was afraid Gamble and company might try to trace it. The last thing he wanted to do was lead them to Gretchen. With that in mind, he stopped at the desk and double-checked to be sure that no information about her whereabouts would be given out.

He walked to a busy street several blocks from the hotel before stopping at a pay phone to call Gamble and get directions to the flat in which the man was staying. It took him about fifteen minutes to catch a cab and he was relieved to note the apartment was nowhere near the hotel where he and Gretchen were staying.

The minute he knocked on the glossy, dark gray door, it opened as if Gamble had been standing there waiting for him. The man's face was bright with excitement and his eyes were avid. "Where is she?" he asked the moment he realized Kurt was alone.

"She isn't with me." Kurt stood just inside the door.

"She isn't with you? Why not?" Gamble's expression alternated between anger and anxiety. "She's here, isn't she? In London, I mean?"

Kurt ignored the question. "What are you going to do if she doesn't want your money?"

Gamble focused on him, seemingly puzzled. "You

mean her inheritance?'' He laughed, but it sounded forced. ''Why wouldn't she want money?''

''She still isn't sure she wants to meet you.''

''She has to meet me!'' Gamble's face flushed. ''I hired you to find her, Miller.''

''Which I did,'' Kurt pointed out. ''But if she doesn't want to meet with you, I can't force her to.''

''She has to!'' Gamble looked furious. ''You don't understand. I promised...I promised her mother I'd look for her.''

''You said the mother was dead.''

''Before she died.'' Gamble was so agitated he was pacing back and forth. Suddenly he stopped in front of Kurt and stabbed a finger into Kurt's chest. It was just a little poke but he didn't like it much.

''It's your job to bring her to us.'' Gamble's voice was shrill. ''We paid you for services and—''

''Who's 'we?'''

''It's just an expression. Don't change the subject.'' His agitation rose again. ''I'll sue you, buddy, if you don't deliver her. I'll—''

''Don't bother.'' Kurt took an envelope from his pocket and slapped it against Gamble's chest. ''Here's your retainer back in full. I don't want the job.''

''You can't do that!'' Gamble practically screamed, but Kurt merely turned and walked back through the still open door. ''You can't do that!'' the man shouted again as Kurt entered the lift and pressed the button for the main floor.

''The hell I can't,'' Kurt muttered. He hailed a cab, vastly relieved to be rid of that duty, but more disturbed than ever by the man's behavior. His subconscious was insistent that something wasn't right about the man's interest in Gretchen, although he still had no proof.

Proof. He took out his cell phone and rapidly punched buttons for an overseas call. He hadn't used it earlier because he didn't want Gamble to get the number.

''Hey,'' he said when Jared Sullivan answered the phone. ''It's your long-lost buddy.''

''You wish.'' Jared's laconic reply masked the affection Kurt knew his friend had a hard time showing.

''Have you got news for me?''

''I do.'' Jared's voice changed. ''Were you hoping these two would be related? Because if you were, you're going to be disappointed. According to my friend in the lab, there's less than a one-in-one-hundred-million chance that there's any genetic linkage.''

''I knew it,'' Kurt said. The confirmation of his fears was both welcome and disturbing. Gamble wanted Gretchen badly, and unless Kurt was mistaken, he wasn't acting alone. The moment he disconnected, he dialed Aiden Swift, with whom he'd finally made contact three days ago. Their conversation was quick and to the point. ''No such person exists,'' Aiden told him. ''I don't know who your client is, but he's definitely not Oliver Gamble.''

He went straight to the university. Once there, a simple query of a guard confirmed that Dr. Wagner was back from Egypt and had come in this afternoon. It was so easy! His blood ran cold as he realized how easily Gamble—or whoever he really was—could find her on his own.

He sat on a bench in the hallway outside her office. He'd walked past once and had seen her engrossed in a thick tome, her attention so focused that she'd never even noticed him. If she didn't notice him, she might not see a lot of other things, either. He didn't know what Gamble wanted with her but the man clearly wasn't entirely sane. She could be kidnapped before she even knew what had happened.

The light in her office finally clicked off around half past six, and he watched as she stepped into the hallway, locking her office door behind her.

Quietly, he stood and stepped very close behind her. When she finally registered his presence, she gasped and whirled, her hands coming up to her throat in instinctive protection.

''Kurt! You scared me to death.'' She frowned. ''What are you doing?''

''Keeping an eye on you.''

''Did you meet with Mr. Gamble today? What's he like? Is he—''

''Whoa. I'll tell you about it over dinner.''

But she shook her head, avoiding his eyes. "I'm having room service tonight. It's been a long day."

"And you didn't get much sleep last night."

Her cheeks turned a delicate shade of pink, but she ignored the comment. "What are you doing here?" she asked again. "I thought you were going to call me when you got back."

"I thought it might be better to come down here and make sure you got back to the hotel safely."

Her eyes widened. He'd forgotten that damnably quick brain of hers. "You met with him and he threatened me, didn't he?" In her agitation, she grasped his arm, the first time she'd willingly touched him since she'd walked away from him that morning.

He hesitated. There was no way to soften it. "He's not your father."

"Did he admit that?"

"No. I sent DNA samples from both of you to a friend of mine. There's no chance you're related. And his name isn't really Oliver Gamble."

"Oh, my God." She stared at him. "So why does he want to meet me so badly?"

"I don't know," said Kurt grimly. "I gave him back his fee and quit. And I'm not leaving your side until we figure this out."

Her face took on that stubborn expression he was quickly coming to detest, her little chin tilting up defiantly, her soft mouth setting in a stubborn line. "I can take care of myself," she said. "You don't need to feel obligated to look after me."

"I don't feel obligated," he said, irritation rising.

"Now that your job is over, you don't need to stick around," she reminded him.

"I know that!" he shouted, goaded out of his calm. "I also know what I *do* need, and if you don't quit arguing with me, we're going into your office and I'll strip you naked so fast you won't know what hit you!"

Her mouth rounded in a perfect *O* of shock. They glared at each other for a moment, eyes clashing. But finally she looked away.

He didn't know whether to be relieved or sorry that she'd backed down. Making love to her on her desk was near the top of his list of fantasies where she was concerned.

As she walked down the hallway without looking back, he stayed right behind her. He wasn't going anywhere until they found out what his former client wanted with his woman.

She looked small and defenseless, strangely fragile as she walked away from him. He wanted to stop her, to take her in his arms and reassure her, but he didn't know what he could say. Because she wanted love and forever, and he knew there was no such thing.

She did her imitation of a stone wall the whole way back to the hotel and in the elevator going up to their floor. As she stepped off and started down the hall, he said, "Will you reconsider having dinner with me this evening?"

She turned and shot him a look of disbelief. ''Not a chance.'' And with that she vanished into her room, leaving him standing in the hallway wondering what it was going to take to get her to admit him back into her life again.

It wasn't that he needed her, he assured himself. He just *wanted* her. There was a difference. And of course, she could be pregnant with his child. He did a quick mental count in his head, wondering how long it would be until she knew and if she'd tell him when she did know for sure.

He sighed, watching the flickering television while lying in his solitary bed. Last night, he'd had Gretchen in his arms, in a bed, beneath him. Where she belonged.

''We have no choice,'' Willard Croft said crisply. ''Thanks to your poor handling of a simple task, Gretchen Wagner isn't going to be convinced to come to us willingly.''

''Kidnapping is a major crime,'' Oliver said nervously. ''I just don't think—''

''That's right,'' said his wife in a contemptuous tone. ''You don't think.'' She glared at him. ''You're talking major crime? *Murder* was a major crime, you idiot!''

''One I didn't want to commit in the first place,'' Oliver flared. ''I'm a scientist, not a thug.''

''You're a failure.'' Agnes dismissed him and

turned back to Croft attentively. "So how would you like us to help?"

Croft snorted. "Just keep *him* away." He gestured to Oliver, who flushed a deep red. "I've got it covered," he said. "She'll be snatched at the university. She has to come out of that office sometime."

Damn! Jake slammed down the phone cursing the myriad tasks he kept adding to his list. He'd been one step behind Gretchen Wagner for nearly two weeks now. Days ago, he'd learned that Gretchen was still in Egypt, but according to the hotel staff, she'd checked out. Where would she go? He had checked over the notes he'd made about the professor's life. She was on temporary assignment at University College London for the semester, during which time she'd gone to Egypt. It stood to reason that she would return to London to finish her work there before returning to Harvard. But he'd called her flat repeatedly without getting an answer. Time to try something else.

Picking up the phone again, he checked his watch even as he dialed. "Yes," he said when a voice asked to be of assistance. "Is Dr. Wagner in her office this morning?"

When the phone rang, Gretchen jumped, then reluctantly reached across the desk to answer it. It was probably Kurt but it could be someone else at the university and she couldn't afford to ignore the call.

"Hello?"

"Is this Dr. Gretchen Wagner?" The voice was a man's, deep and confident. It was a nice voice, and instinctively she warmed to it.

"Yes, it is."

"Dr. Wagner..." The man hesitated. "My name is Jake. Jake Ingram." He stopped again and she had the distinct impression that he wanted the name to mean something to her.

"Yes, Mr. Ingram?"

"I'm— You might be— Damn! Sorry," he said quickly. "This is more difficult than I'd thought."

She was intrigued, and just a little alarmed. "What is?"

The man with the compelling voice sighed. "Gretchen, I know this is going to be hard for you to believe, but I'm pretty sure I'm your brother."

"My brother!" It was the last thing she'd expected and she was stunned. Beyond stunned. "I was told I didn't have a brother. But I've had dreams about having several brothers, and a sister. Why do you think we're related?"

"Just hear me out," he said hurriedly. "Were you adopted when you were twelve?"

"Yes." She was too shocked to dissemble.

"And do you have little or no memory of your early life?"

"A little," she said cautiously.

"And if your academic position is any indication, you're exceptionally intelligent with a gift for linguistics, right?"

"Yes." She'd gotten blasé about her unusual intellect years ago.

"There are reasons for all of those things," he told her. "I believe you and I are brother and sister. In fact, we're twins."

She couldn't even answer him. Twins! She didn't know this man from Adam but as soon as she'd heard his voice, she'd felt he was no danger to her. And what he was telling her… While it was a shock, there was something inside her, something deep and certain, that affirmed what she'd just heard.

"Gretchen?"

"Jake." She swallowed. "My brother."

"You believe me?"

She gave a choked laugh. "I shouldn't, but…I do. I believe you. When I heard your voice, something inside me knew, I think."

"We have to get together," he said.

"Yes! I'd love that. I'll be back in the States within the week. Where are you?" she asked.

"Texas," he said. "I live here, although I travel extensively."

"Are you married?" *Do I have other relatives?*

"No. Are you?"

"No." The whole awful situation with Kurt leaped into her mind and she fell silent.

"Okay." He seemed to sense her sudden depression. "I'd like to see you right away. Could I fly to London and meet with you there?"

"Right away?" She could hardly believe it. "That would be wonderful."

"Great," he said. "Dinner tomorrow evening?"

She laughed, disbelieving. "You're kidding."

"Not in the least."

"I'd like that." She hesitated. "It's so weird that you would contact me right now. There's a man who wants me to meet him as well. He claims he's my father."

"Your *father?*" Jake sounded taken aback. No, more than that. He sounded absolutely floored.

"Well, he claimed to be my father," she said, "but I don't believe he really is."

"How did you get in contact with this guy?"

"He contacted me. He recognized me from a *National Geographic* article."

"Probably the same one I saw."

"He hired a private investigator to find me."

"But you haven't met him yet?"

"No." She hesitated. "I've had a funny feeling about him. I can't explain it. In any case, the private investigator says he's lying—"

"I thought the investigator was working for the guy hunting you." Jake's mind evidently worked as fast as her own.

"He does. Or he did. He quit," she said. "After we met he realized that some things didn't make sense and started checking them out."

"For you."

"Well, yes."

"I think I see." Jake's voice held amusement. But it quickly vanished as he said, "What's his name?"

"Kurt Miller. He's from Texas."

"Not the P.I. The guy who says he's your father."

"Gamble, Oliver Gamble." Was she imagining it, or did she hear Jake suck in a quick hiss of air?

"Gretchen." The sudden intensity in his voice was unnerving. "Whatever you do, please don't meet with that man until I get to London and speak with you."

"All right." She was surprised at how relieved she was to have yet another reason to stay away from Oliver Gamble. "But, Jake, I think we should talk to him at some point. Even if he isn't our father—"

"He isn't. Trust me."

"He has some knowledge of our childhood. He must have known us when we were small." Her voice grew plaintive. "He might be my best hope of ever knowing why I was given away."

"Gretchen." Her brother's voice was incredibly tender. "You weren't given up by choice. I've met our mother. She's still alive and I can tell you everything she's shared with me. In fact, I know she'll be thrilled that I've found you. Just promise me you won't meet that man. He's dangerous. I'll explain it all when I see you."

Dangerous? This couldn't be her life they were discussing, could it? Until the past few weeks, the most exciting thing that had ever happened to her had been the opportunity to work on the Ahk Tablets. Her life had been beyond bland. "I promise." Her head was spinning. First a father, now a brother and a mother showed up. It had to be more than coincidence.

Twelve

He was waiting for her outside her hotel room door in the morning, and Gretchen cast him a jaundiced eye. "Don't you ever sleep?"

"I'd have slept better if you'd been in my arms."

As Kurt had expected, she ignored the comment.

He fell into step beside her. "What are we doing today? I haven't eaten yet."

"I have," she said repressively. "And I'm going to work today. You've been entertaining yourself for years, keep it up."

He refused to let her brush him off. "Okay. I brought a book. I'll hang out on that little bench where I sat yesterday."

She looked truly aghast. "No! You can't do that again."

"Sure I can. It isn't that bad." He deliberately misunderstood her. "Although one of those big wing chairs in your office probably would be more comfortable."

"I don't want you there." She planted her feet and faced him.

"Tough. I'm staying until you're ready to leave

and then we can have dinner in some great little pub tonight."

"I have plans for dinner already."

"With who?" It slipped out before he could catch it. She was shy, he reminded himself, not friendless. And she was back in London, where she'd been many times before. She probably had a lot of contacts scattered around the area.

"None of your business."

"It could be. You have no idea what Gamble wants, but he's clearly ready to go to extraordinary lengths to get it."

She sighed. "I'm having dinner with my brother, if you must know."

"Your brother?"

She nodded. "He called me yesterday."

His hair was standing on end. How naive could one person be? "Gretchen..." He reached for patience. "How do you know this person is your brother? Have you ever met him? A month ago you didn't think you even had any biological siblings."

The chin came up. "It's hard to explain."

"Try."

She glared at him. "Not if you're going to be rude. Besides, this is none of your business."

He swallowed. She was on the verge of walking away from him and he knew he couldn't let that happen. Humbly he said, "I promise I won't be rude. I'd really like to hear about your brother."

She was still glaring at him. "Whom you don't believe really could be my brother."

"I'll keep an open mind."

Suspicion was written all over her face.

"Please," he said quietly.

Still she stared at him, and the look on her face slowly eased from doubt into vulnerability. "Why?" she whispered.

"Something's wrong." He took a deep breath, desperate to convince her. "You're in danger. I can't prove it, but I know it as sure as we're standing here. The more I know about anyone who contacts you, the better able I am to take care of you."

Ten minutes ago he knew she would have said, "I don't need you to take care of me." But now, as her wide blue eyes gauged his sincerity, she said, "All right. I got a telephone call yesterday at my office from a man named Jake Ingram."

"Jake Ingram!"

"Do you know him?"

"Not personally, but I certainly know of him. Haven't you ever heard the name? He's got fingers in practically every financial pie around the globe. He's known for that alone, but a couple months ago, his adopted brother was kidnapped and there was some speculation that the real target of the kidnapping was Ingram."

"Oh, no. What happened to the brother?"

"He escaped. Don't worry, he's fine. Ingram also is working closely with the FBI to solve the World

Bank Heist. His name is in the news practically every day."

She shook her head. "Sorry. If it doesn't involve languages or classical studies I probably have seen it without ever absorbing a thing."

He smiled wryly. "You do have a single-minded streak."

She didn't return the expression. "Is that a bad thing?"

"No," he said hastily. "Not at all. It's part of your charm."

She looked dubious, but didn't comment.

"So," he said, "a man claiming to be Jake Ingram contacted you and told you what?"

"He said he was pretty sure he was my brother," she confessed. "My twin brother. He seemed to know a lot about me."

"Did he know anything that he couldn't have found out through public channels? Think," he urged.

She did. "No, I suppose he didn't," she said reluctantly after a moment. "He did tell me that my mother is alive, that she didn't give me up willingly, although he didn't give details. He said he would do that when we met."

"Which is when?"

"Dinner this evening."

He gritted his teeth. "After what we learned about Gamble, you just agreed to have dinner with a total stranger?"

She hesitated. "Kurt, don't laugh at this, but when I heard his voice, it felt right. I'm almost certain Jake Ingram is my brother."

"You also thought Gamble was your father."

"But I never wanted to meet him," she said. "Something about the whole situation gave me the willies. That's why I kept delaying. And after what Jake said about Gamble, I realize my instincts were sound."

"Ingram knows about Gamble?" He rubbed his forehead.

"He made me promise not to meet with Gamble until after we'd had dinner and a chance to talk. He says Gamble is dangerous."

"That I can believe. So this person who says he's Ingram is coming here today."

"This evening."

"Well," he said, "there's one good thing about this—I know what Ingram looks like. I'll be able to tell if it's him or not."

"You're not coming to dinner with us." Her soft tone was as intractable as if they'd never had a thaw moments earlier.

He had a sudden mental image of her with a strange man, of her being bundled into a car against her will, and he was totally panicked again. How the hell could he keep her safe if she insisted on doing dumb things like this? The sixth sense he'd always relied on was screaming "Danger!" and although he couldn't prove it, he was certain that something was very wrong in this whole situation.

Frustration overcame his determination to handle her carefully. "Don't be stupid," he exploded. "Can't you see what you're doing? You're so blinded by your desire to find your roots that you're taking foolish, unnecessary chances."

She rocked back as if he'd slapped her. "*I'm* blind?" It was a furious whisper. Even in her anger, she was loath to make a scene in the hallway. "You're a good one to talk. Your whole life is hobbled by the limits you set on yourself. You have this deep, dark secret from the past and you won't even share it. I'm shut out because of your fear of...what? Failure? Being hurt? Being left again?" Her tone was scornful. "You're a great big coward who refuses to take a chance on a future with me because you can't let go of your past."

He was stunned. Her words cascaded over him, worming their way into his mind, and he couldn't hide from the truth of them.

She stepped back and opened her door again, then entered her room alone. The door closed with a resounding bang, and still he stood there.

Your whole life is hobbled by the limits you set on yourself.

Could she be right? An arrow of truth pierced the protective shell he'd kept in place. Of course she could.

But *was* she? He was afraid she was. He'd given

those years in Prince George's County an enormous amount of power over the rest of his life by allowing himself to give in to the fears those years had engendered.

Fears of trusting someone who might not be utterly trustworthy. Fears of letting someone get close, only to turn and walk away.

It was time to let go of his past. It was human to make mistakes. He'd made as many as anyone else in those long-ago days. But letting himself be ruled by a determination not to let anyone get close was as big a mistake as Karey had made in putting a career over the life they could have made together.

To his surprise, he realized he didn't think of her with bitterness anymore. How could he? He didn't have room to think of any woman but Gretchen.

Gretchen. His very real fears for her safety came flooding back. She needed him. Couldn't she see that?

She could get herself hurt—or even killed. The thought stopped him in his tracks. God, what would he do without her? His chest felt like it was being squeezed in a giant vise.

In a moment of perfect clarity, he saw how stupid he'd been. He loved her. *He loved her.* He loved her stubborn little chin, her incredible mind, her long, slim body. He loved the way her eyes went wide and dark when he kissed her, the way her hand felt in his, how she fit perfectly into his arms when they danced together.

And he wanted—no, he *needed*—to spend the rest of his life with her.

And then fear struck. She'd told him she loved him and he'd told her no thanks. What if she had changed her mind? He wanted to believe that she couldn't just fall out of love with him with as easily as snapping a finger, but Karey had done exactly that when her career had been threatened by her association with him.

But Gretchen wasn't Karey, he reminded himself. Gretchen was infinitely more capable of thinking for herself. Gretchen had gone her own way all her life. She wasn't the kind of person to be swayed by what others thought.

But the possibility still remained that he might have hurt her too badly to reclaim what he'd tossed away. He hammered back the panicky feeling. She still loved him. He was almost certain of it. Somehow, there had to be a way to get her to give him a second chance.

Gretchen wiped her palms nervously against the serviceable fabric of her suit skirt. She had butterflies in her stomach big enough to carry her back to the States. In fact, she felt slightly sick.

Was Kurt right? Was she crazy to be doing this? How did she know Jake Ingram was really her brother, or that the man coming to meet her was really even Jake Ingram?

But hearing his voice had *felt* right, she reminded

herself. It sounded ridiculous when she tried to explain it, but he had felt right. As right as Gamble had felt wrong, and she'd never even heard his voice.

She glanced at her watch. Seven on the dot. Maybe he wouldn't show. Maybe—

She glanced at the entrance to the restaurant she'd chosen and there he was. Her brother. Jake. There was no doubt in her mind. Not a single one. She still didn't know how she knew him, but she did.

The boy she remembered had had a shock of dark hair, piercing blue eyes and a deep tan from their endless hours out in the North Carolina sun.

North Carolina? She realized she'd just had another piece of her childhood fall into place.

The man walking toward her still resembled the boy, although the hair was significantly shorter and he was much bigger than she'd expected. The blue eyes met hers and crinkled into a smile, and suddenly she was rushing toward him.

He held out his arms and she hugged him hard, without reservation. "It's really you," she said, and she realized she was crying.

"I remember you," he said. "I remember you!" There was a note of wonder in his voice, and the realization that she wasn't the only one whose memory had been impaired made her draw back in shock.

"You have trouble remembering things, too? That's weird." Her brain was racing a mile a minute. "Even if you suffered the same traumatic shock

I did, the odds that you would lose your memories must be—''

''Whoa!'' Her brother was laughing. ''I can see we're going to have a lot of things to talk about.'' He turned her and walked to the reservation desk. ''Two for Ingram.''

She registered the note of authority, the carriage of his body that said he clearly expected his wishes to be followed. ''Right this way, Mr. Ingram,'' the maître d' said. ''We've reserved a quiet table for you as you requested.''

At the table, they were seated and Jake ordered drinks before sitting back and looking across the table at her. ''Ah,'' he said with a sigh, ''our mother was right. You *do* look a lot like her.''

Our mother. Her throat grew tight and she felt the sting of tears. Bowing her head, she waited for the moment to pass. ''Did you grow up with her?''

Jake looked startled. ''No! No longer than you. We all were placed in adoptive homes.''

''Five of us?'' she whispered.

He nodded. ''Do you remember them?''

''No names, not much more than a family scene on the beach. Two younger brothers and a sister, and you, me, Mom and Dad. And another couple. Maybe an aunt and uncle?''

He let that pass. ''You and I are twins,'' he told her. ''There was a third child—a boy—who died at birth. The little kids also are triplets.''

Her mind immediately thought about the long odds of that happening. "That's really unusual."

"Not for us," Jake said grimly. He took a sip of his drink. "This is a wild story," he told her. "You're going to think I'm crazy, but let me tell you what Violet—that's our mother's name—told me. Then we can compare notes on what we remember."

"All right."

"Before we start," Jake said, "there's a big, dark-haired guy sitting on the other side of the room who's watching you like a hawk. Anyone you know?"

Gretchen couldn't resist the compulsion to squirm around in her seat and look. Kurt was staring right at her, and when their eyes met, she felt herself blush. Quickly she turned back around to face her brother's speculative expression. "He's the private investigator I told you about."

"I thought you said he quit."

"He did." When Jake's eyebrows rose, she sighed. "It's...complicated. He won't go away until he's sure I'm safe."

"Isn't he the one who realized Grimble wasn't really your father?"

She was sure she looked as blank as she felt. "Grimble? Do you mean Mr. Gamble?"

Jake nodded. "His real name is Oliver Grimble. He...knew us when we were little."

"What does he want?"

"Us," Jake said. "Listen, would you mind if I

invite your guy to join us? If he's going to look after you anyway, he might as well be in the loop.''

''I suppose so,'' she said hesitantly. Then his words penetrated. ''He's not my guy.''

''Right. Would you like to invite him to join us?''

It wasn't really a request so much as it was a command, she realized. Reluctantly she rose to her feet. ''No, but you're probably right. If you tell both of us at once, it'll save me from having to repeat it later. Kurt's like a pit bull once he decides he wants something...he just sinks his teeth in and hangs on.''

''And are you something he wants?''

She shook her head. ''Not really.'' She couldn't have smiled for a million dollars. And she walked away while Jake was puzzling over that.

Kurt felt his pulse pick up as Gretchen rose from the table where she'd been sitting and came toward him. She was lithe and quietly lovely, her blue eyes fixed on the floor. Her face was sober and he wondered how much he'd be willing to pay to see her smile at him in that intimate way that had warmed his heart even when he hadn't been willing to admit it.

''My brother would like you to join us,'' she said without preamble when she reached him.

''And how about you?''

She shrugged. ''You might as well. Otherwise, I know you'll just bug me until I repeat every detail.''

He tilted his head, studying her unhappy face.

"Gretchen," he said quietly, "if you don't want me there, it's all right."

She hesitated, shrugged again. "I don't care."

Recognizing that that was the best he was going to get from her at the moment, Kurt rose from his chair and donned the jacket he'd hung over its back.

"Wait a minute," she said, frustration evident in her voice. "No snide comment? No telling me I'm stupid for thinking he might be my brother?"

Kurt smiled slightly. "No. Seeing the two of you together, there's no doubt in my mind that you're related. You have the same eyes, but more than that, you share mannerisms, qualities that can't be easily described, that practically shout it."

He'd been in his chair before they ever entered the restaurant after he'd ascertained that a Jake Ingram had a reservation that evening. After positively identifying the man as Jake Ingram, Kurt had surveyed the restaurant. He was fairly certain the couple at the next table who had come in immediately after them were bodyguards. He'd caught the sidelong glances directed at Jake as well as the dedicated manner in which both the man and the woman constantly scanned their surroundings.

Observing Gretchen and her companion, he was mildly amazed by the similarities they shared, even though they didn't look exactly alike. They both had a distinctive manner of dragging their hair away from their faces, though in Jake's case it was out of habit rather than necessity. The way they tilted their heads when listening intently, certain hand motions they made...they even walked a bit alike, with shoulders back and a self-confident air that proclaimed these were people with a purpose.

It was damned strange, he decided. Then he realized that maybe it wasn't so strange after all—they were raised together until they were twelve. And that was perhaps the strangest thing of all: He was utterly and completely sure that Jake Ingram and Gretchen Wagner were brother and sister.

"Well," she said, clearly at a loss for a good comeback, "that's something."

He followed her across the room.

The other man stood at his approach and held out a hand. Kurt clasped it firmly, assessing from the grip he received in return that Jake Ingram had no intention of showing weakness. Not that he'd expected it; the man's reputation for solid, unyielding tactics in his business dealings was well-known around the globe.

After the introductions were complete and Kurt had been seated, Jake said, "I understand you've been face-to-face with the man you know as Oliver Gamble."

Kurt nodded.

"Is this the same man?" Jake took a photo from his breast pocket and laid it on the table.

Kurt nodded again. "That's him. Have you met him?"

Jake nodded. "This photo was taken at an event I

attended in Texas. It was just coincidental that he was in one of the crowd shots, but I got a copy after I realized who he was."

Gretchen leaned over and picked up the picture, turning it so she could see it. The moment she got a good look at it, though, she dropped it as if it had burned her hand. Her face went white.

"Gretchen, what's wrong?" Kurt was out of his chair in an instant, kneeling at her side and encircling her in his arm. She felt delicate and fragile, and a wave of protectiveness swamped him as he stroked her upper arm soothingly through her suit jacket.

"I don't know." She indicated the photograph. "I just got the strongest feeling of...revulsion when I looked at him." She pointed a shaking finger at herself and Jake. "That man is *not* our father."

"No," Jake said soberly. "He's not. Our father is dead. And Violet is pretty certain that this man and his wife killed him."

"Who's Violet?" Kurt asked. He dragged his chair over to Gretchen's side, sitting close and keeping her against him.

Jake rubbed his forehead. "All right. Let me start at the beginning." He went on to relate a story about a special project in genetic engineering in the sixties, about the CIA and rogue agents, about children—now grown—with diverse abilities so extraordinary that whoever controlled them would command such power that they could probably disrupt the entire world as it currently existed.

The whole thing sounded so fantastic Kurt would have had trouble believing it under normal circumstances—except that two of the supposedly genetically engineered children were sitting right here at this table. Additionally, for weeks already he'd subconsciously suspected Gretchen's background might include elements of those wild tabloid rumors. He did his best not to stare at Jake. If he and Gretchen were typical examples, Kurt had little doubt that each of the other siblings also possessed far more than simply slightly unusual abilities.

"So there are five of you," he said to Jake. "And you believe the Achilles behind the World Bank Heist is your brother Gideon?"

Jake nodded. "They're controlling him. And Violet and I believe that the purpose of that heist is to secure funds to help them continue the search for Faith and Mark."

Kurt's mind was reeling. "They aren't going to get Gretchen." He put his free hand over hers where they were clutched together in her lap, and was gratified when she didn't pull away. "Your real name is Grace," he said. "Does that sound familiar?"

But she shook her head. "I don't know. There are more thoughts in my head than water droplets in the ocean right now."

"Is there anything we can do about the memory loss?" Kurt glanced across the table to Jake Ingram, who was eyeing them with a slight smile.

The smile faded and Jake shrugged. "I don't know

yet. I'm going to have to talk to some experts. My adoptive brother Zach's fiancée is a psychiatrist who specializes in hypnosis. Maisy may be able to help us figure out what they did to us to repress our memories. I think it almost has to be some kind of hypnosis."

"But tinkering with your minds without knowing exactly what we're doing might be more harmful than helpful." No way was Kurt going to allow anyone to do anything to damage Gretchen's marvelous mind.

Jake clearly understood his point. "I would never let anyone harm her," he said. He looked at Gretchen. "It sounds as if you remember a little more than I do. And what I do recall is...I don't know, shrouded or something, just bits and pieces that aren't connected."

Gretchen nodded. "That's how I feel. It's like condensation on glass. Every once in a while a drop slides down and clears the view for a moment, then it mists over again."

"I'm willing to bet the other kids have the same kinds of memory problems."

Gretchen shook her head. "I'm having trouble wrapping my mind around the fact that I've got four siblings. And a mother." Her voice held awe.

"So I presume the next task is to locate the missing kids," Kurt said.

"Before our buddy Grimble and his boss Willard Croft do," Jake added.

"Tell me what you need me to do," Kurt said.

Jake looked at him, at the woman cradled in his arm and said, "Just keep my sister safe for now. Give me a day or two to talk to my contact at the FBI."

"All right." Kurt jerked his head to indicate the couple at the next table. "Bodyguards?"

Jake nodded. "Yeah. You're sharp. I can offer you some help if you need it."

Kurt considered the notion. He had no intention of leaving Gretchen unprotected. But he badly wanted to check out Grimble's flat again. "All right. Let me know when you've set it up." The two men exchanged cell phone numbers and Jake handed him an additional card with nothing but a number printed on it. "If anything happens to me, call this number and ask for Lennox. He'll help Gretchen."

"Lennox."

"Nothing's going to happen to any of us." Gretchen sounded alarmed. "Is it?"

"No." Kurt stroked her shoulder again. "We're going to find your brothers and sister and get these guys."

But as he looked over her head into her brother's eyes, he knew it wasn't going to be as simple as that. Their adversaries had literally had years to plot and plan. God only knew what they might attempt next.

Thirteen

Kurt escorted her back to her room with his arm around her waist. Gretchen was so overwhelmed by all her brother's information that she didn't even protest. She knew she should still be mad at Kurt, but for the life of her she couldn't work up the energy when all her conscious thoughts were trying to assimilate the fact that she had living family members, a mother who was anxious to talk with her and a twin brother.

When they reached her door, Kurt took her key from her hand and silently opened the door, then stepped inside and flipped on the lights. He checked the bathroom and the closet before coming back to her side, and it wasn't until then that she realized what he was doing.

"You're checking for bad guys." She knew that was a less-than-adequate phrase, but her brain was humming with so many notions, it was a wonder she could speak at all.

"Um-hmm." He came to stand in front of her.

"You're not a bodyguard," she said. "You're a private investigator."

"I'm *your* bodyguard," he said gently. He put his hands on her shoulders and gently squeezed, and she imagined he could feel the tension. "And as such, I prescribe a hot shower and a massage."

She looked up at him, her eyes heavy with fatigue. "Doctors prescribe. Bodyguards guard."

He set his hands at the lapels of her suit jacket and gently tugged it off, tossing it onto the desk chair before he returned his attentions to her. His fingers settled at the top button of her shirt and slipped the small button through its hole.

"I can do that myself," she objected, but there was no conviction in her tone.

"Let me." He spoke quietly, soothingly.

She put her hands up around his wrists, intending to protest, but she couldn't quite seem to form the words. So instead, she simply stood there, pathetically docile and compliant, as he pushed her blouse from her shoulders and unzipped her skirt. It fell around her ankles and she stepped out of it and her shoes at the same time.

Now she wore only her bra and panties beneath the panty hose he was already rolling down her legs, and she put a hand on his shoulder to steady herself.

"Kurt?" she said faintly.

"Shh." He tossed the panty hose onto the growing pile atop the chair and rose, laying a finger over her lips. "There will be time to talk tomorrow." Then he drew her into his arms, rocking her slightly from side to side for a moment, his big hands more gentle than she would ever have believed.

Her head fell forward to rest against his chest and she rubbed her cheek against the hard planes through his shirt. He caught her hand and carried it up to his collar. "Undress me," he said.

Gretchen stilled. She knew what he was asking and she realized that she had a choice to make now. She could send him away or she could accept what they had between them, even if Kurt didn't want to admit it existed. Then she became aware of the tension in his body. He was like a statue, but beneath the surface he was vibrating with concealed anxiety. And oddly enough, that was what decided her.

He might not admit he needed her, but he did. Someone had hurt him. Some woman. She didn't know details, but she didn't need them. She had enough love to heal him, she was sure, if he could allow himself to trust her with his heart. All she had to do was wait. And love him.

She lifted her other hand and began to undo the buttons of his dress shirt while he swiftly opened his cuffs. He shrugged it off while she pulled handfuls of his T-shirt up, and then he took that, too, pulling it over his head and throwing it aside.

The heavy mat of dark fur on his chest drew her, and she combed her fingers through it, finding and exploring the flat copper nipples. He was getting hard so fast the fabric of his pants was drawn tight over him and when she opened his belt, unbuttoned them and pulled down his zipper, he sighed with relief and pleasure at the soft brush of her palms over his erection. Then she slipped her hands beneath the band of his briefs. She slid around until she was cupping his tight buttocks as she worked the pants down and they fell around his ankles.

She was so close that one step sandwiched him against her warm belly. He let his head drop back with a groan as his hips moved against her involuntarily. Her small fingers traced the crease of his buttocks until he shuddered and pulled her hands away.

"You're tired," he said. "Shower. Then bed." He pulled off his socks, then led her into the bathroom and removed her bra and panties. Then he turned on the shower until the water was warm and comfortable before he lifted her into the cubicle. She'd grabbed a barrette and clipped up her hair while he fooled with the water temperature, and she made a small sound of pleasure as the warm water cascaded over her sensitive skin.

He started to back away, but she put her fingers around his wrist and tugged. "You, too."

He hesitated. "I don't think that's a good idea. You don't need—"

Gretchen reached down between them and her small hand closed around his rigid, straining shaft. "I need you," she said.

Without another word he stepped into the shower behind her. He reached up to angle the hot spray so that it beat down on her shoulders and back. At the same time he was massaging her shoulders, stroking and squeezing, digging his thumbs firmly into the tense cords that ran along her spine, working out every knot he found. She groaned a little as he worked. "That feels so good," she said.

She swayed closer to him as he worked, feeling the brush of his erection against her bottom, enjoying the anticipation that shortened her breath and sent quivers of desire arrowing down between her legs.

As the painful tension faded, it was replaced by a much more pleasurable neediness. Kurt's hands slowed; languidly he slipped them around her rib cage until he found her breasts, and when he cupped them in his hands, she leaned back against him.

Kurt groaned, his thumbs flicking lightly over her nipples. Her head fell back against his shoulder, and he quickly reached up and turned off the shower. The motion rubbed him against her, and she lifted herself on tiptoe, then rolled down onto her heels, sliding up and down and repeating the action as she pressed her bottom back against him.

"You're killing me." His voice was thick and guttural, almost unrecognizable. "The hell with the bed," he said hoarsely.

Abruptly, he spun her around so fast she cried out and clutched at him. He lifted her almost in the same motion, and Gretchen gasped as she felt his erection pushing at the junction of her thighs at the same time as her back hit the cool tiles of the shower stall.

"Open your legs," he whispered, and the moment

she complied, she felt him pushing, prodding, his hips relentlessly working until her soft flesh admitted him into her body. "Oh, yeah," he said as she felt the broad tip penetrate her. "Look."

She glanced up at him, but he smiled, more a grimace than a true smile, and dropped his gaze along the length of their bodies. Her eyes followed his. He was thick and hard, his shaft a deep, dark red where it jutted from the nest of dark curls. Her hips were close to his, a breath separating them, and she could see where he disappeared into her own dark cloud of hair. As she watched, he slipped his hands under her bottom and pulled her closer, and she gasped as she felt him drive deeply into her at the same time she watched her body fully accept him.

Kurt threw his head back and without thinking she stretched up to kiss the taut column of his throat. The action tilted her hips forward, seating him to the hilt inside her, rubbing his hard body against the ultrasensitive, throbbing locus of pleasure that quivered at the very edge of her stretched, slippery opening.

He glanced down at her with knowing eyes and a tight smile on his face as he took her hips in his big hands and held her in place. Slowly, he began to move. She clamped her ankles around his waist, trying to hold him in place, but he withdrew almost completely from her before plunging forward again abruptly. Her breath caught in her throat. He repeated the action again and again, and each time she flew closer to the edge of the cliff until finally she uttered a short, strangled scream as sharp jolts of unbearable pleasure exploded in her core, sending out shock waves that shook her entire body.

Kurt's body started as if he'd received an electrical shock and his hips moved against her, withdrawing and then plunging forward, moving faster and faster, hammering at her as she hung suspended in the grip of the overwhelming, earth-shattering climax that went on and on. She was with him every step of the way until, with a deep shudder that arched his back and pushed him even deeper inside her, she felt the warm pulses of his release jetting against her inner walls. Finally his rigid muscles began to relax, bit by bit, and his head dropped forward to rest over hers. Both their bodies slumped against the wall.

"Damn," he said with deep feeling.

She agreed completely.

When he finally stepped back and lifted her off him, he turned the shower on again. He quickly and efficiently washed them both off. She made a small sound when his soapy hand slipped between her legs, but he didn't linger and had her body washed and rinsed within moments. She felt a little tug of embarrassment when he put a hand on her inner thigh and spread her legs so he could gently blot the water away, and she must have made some sound, because he smiled as he finished drying her and tossed the towel over the bar.

Then he lifted her into his arms and carried her to her bed, setting her down and tugging back the covers. She slid between the cool sheets and only realized he intended to join her when he gently pushed her over and got in beside her.

When he turned to her and held out his arms, she didn't hesitate. They might not have resolved her feelings, or his, but she couldn't fight her need for him tonight.

The last thought she had before she fell asleep was that he hadn't used a condom this time, either. But her brain was too fatigued to puzzle that one out, though she thought there was something she was missing....

He woke in the middle of the night, thirsty, and slid out of the bed without waking her. He walked into the bathroom and drank his fill, then came back through the dark, his eyes adjusting so that he had no trouble negotiating by the dim light that seeped in around the edge of the heavy curtains. In his absence, Gretchen had rolled to her back. The sheet rode low around her hips, exposing the trim contours of her body. One arm was outflung, the other bonelessly draped between her pretty breasts.

He could no more stay away from her—now or ever—than he could stop breathing.

Putting a knee on the bed, he parted her thighs and knelt between them. Just seeing her lying there had been enough to get him hard again, and he guided himself to her, nudging at the entrance to her body.

''Mmm.'' She stirred but didn't even open her

eyes, simply lifted her arms and twined them about his neck, her fingers sliding into his hair and her nails gently scraping his scalp. The sensation sent chills chasing down his spine, but as he recalled his almost-embarrassing record-speed performance in the bathroom a few hours before, he was determined not to rush this time.

Slowly he entered her and lowered his weight onto her. He reached down and drew her legs up, hooking his arms beneath her knees so that he was pressed hard against her, then began thrusting slowly as he found her mouth and plunged his tongue deeply inside, searching out the hidden sweetness as her own tongue curled around his in erotic invitation.

In and out, deep and shallow, he kept up the leisurely pace for long moments as she gripped his forearms. Eventually, she began to make small whimpering noises in rhythm with his motion, and the little sounds turned him on even more. She was straining against him and he released her legs, slipping his hands beneath her and tilting her pelvis up to take him more deeply.

Then a thought occurred to him, interrupting his concentration on her pleasure and his own. It was important enough that he stopped moving altogether for a moment, savoring the tight, clinging feeling where her body gripped his shaft. She looked up at him. "What's wrong?"

He shook his head. "Nothing." Then he said, "I'm not using anything."

"I know." Her voice was sober and quiet, unrevealing.

"I'm not going to start, either," he informed her.

Her eyes widened. "All right," she said faintly.

Propping himself on his elbows and cupping her face with his hands, he dropped his head and found her mouth, kissing her long and deep. Finally, she wrenched her head away and said, "I have to breathe!"

He chuckled, and she said, "Ooh, do that again."

That made him laugh harder and she wriggled with pleasure. God, he was happy. He felt lighter than he had in years, buoyant with the goodness of his life.

Looking down at her, he said, "I love you."

As the words sank in, he felt her whole body go slack with shock. "Wh—what?"

"I love you," he repeated. As her eyes filled with tears, he kissed her slowly, reverently. "I've got to be the stupidest man on the face of the earth—"

"Amen to that." It was said with feeling.

"Hey!" He kissed her harder, making it last when she wrapped her arms around his neck and clung.

"Tell me again," she demanded when he finally lifted his head.

"I love you," he said promptly. And then, diffidently, "And I wouldn't mind hearing it back."

"You know I love you." She frowned, and there was the memory of hurt in her eyes. "It's not like something I can turn on and off at will. I will love you every day of my life."

He closed his eyes and rested his forehead against hers, relief and regret mingling inside him. "I was sure I ruined everything."

"I could never stop loving you," she said and there was a deep tenderness in her tone.

"I'm sorry," he said. "I'm sorry I reacted the way I did. I just had my life set in concrete. I was never expecting you to come along and I wasn't ready to let myself take a chance."

"I understand." Her voice was quiet and her fingers stroked the back of his neck in a gentle caress.

He began moving again, telling her how much he loved her with each stroke, treasuring the feel of her slim body in his arms. When he was on fire, straining to stay in control, he reached down between their bodies and put his thumb at the top of her sweet mound, exposing the tiny swollen nubbin and rubbing relentlessly until she came, bucking and screaming beneath him. Only then did he release the tight rein on his self-control. The moment his body recognized its freedom, he felt the impossible tension that preceded his release drawing him taut, and then hurling him into climax. She held his shuddering body and he poured himself into her in deep, throbbing pulses that finally left him spent and exhausted. Eventually, he realized he had to move or he'd crush her. He dragged himself off her and drew her into his arms, kissing her temple as sleep claimed them both.

* * *

In the morning they showered together, then ordered a room-service breakfast. As they ate, Kurt looked across the small table at Gretchen. Her face was positively glowing. No man alive would mistake that look of pleasured satisfaction for anything other than a woman who'd been well loved last night. He felt himself grow aroused at the mere memory, and had to muster his self-control.

He finished his last bite of toast, then went to his own room for fresh clothing. Soon after, Gretchen left to head for the university; he intended to meet her there very soon.

But first, he wanted to see if Grimble was still hanging around London. He was planning to take a taxi over to the flat where he'd met the man and see what he could find out.

He was heading across the lobby toward the taxi stand when something about the familiar shape of an iron-gray head in a wing chair stopped him in his tracks. Quickly, Kurt detoured around a column where the man couldn't see him and made his way around a stand of potted trees with long, exotic-looking leaves until he was within six feet of the fellow.

Obscured as he was, he still had a decent view through a break in the fringed leaves. And as he zeroed in on the gray-haired man, his blood froze. *It was Grimble!*

The man was on a cell phone. Kurt could hear

every word spoken and he listened in mounting horror as comprehension dawned.

"She just left the hotel," Grimble said. "Getting into a taxi, headed in the direction of the university. She never goes anywhere else—she's the original old maid." His voice was contemptuous. "I'm sure that's where she's headed."

Grimble fell silent, then spoke again. "All right. Once you have her, I'll meet you there."

Kurt didn't move, although he badly wanted to get his hands around the man's scrawny neck. Hidden by the large fronds of the tree, he rapidly weighed his limited options. He could grab Grimble and force him to reveal the location where they were taking Gretchen. But that was risky. What if Grimble wouldn't talk or Kurt arrived too late and they moved her somewhere else? Not to mention that she'd be completely traumatized by a kidnapping.

He was already moving back the way he'd come, his decision made as he went. If Gretchen had just left the hotel a few moments ago, he probably had just enough time to get to UCL ahead of her. His best bet would be to prevent her being snatched at all.

He dialed Jake as he slipped from behind the tree and bolted for the entrance. He waved his arm frantically for a taxi and thanked the gods of traffic when one pulled over almost immediately. Giving the driver the address of UCL and instructions to get there by the fastest roads possible, he jumped into the back seat. Just as he did, he heard Jake's recorded voice pick up and instruct him to leave a message.

"Dammit!" he said, uncaring that Jake would catch that as well. "I'm on my way to UCL. I overheard Grimble talking to someone who's there in position to abduct Gretchen." He set his jaw and willed himself to calm down. "I'll die before I let them take her," he said quietly. "Get there if you can."

Disconnecting, he slid the phone into his pocket and sat in tense silence as the driver careened down alleys and roared through warning signals, cutting minutes off the normally leisurely drive. Once the driver pulled to a stop, he jumped out and fell in step behind three coeds who were strolling along the sidewalk that led to the main entrance.

Just ahead of him, he saw a taxi pull up. As it paused there, a man came into view from the right, walking fast. He was wearing jeans and a sweatshirt but he was clearly a lot older than the average university attendee. The door of the car opened and Gretchen's slim legs in her practical black pumps swung into view. She stood, turning to thank the driver.

The man in the sweatshirt was running now, and Kurt began to run as well, sprinting around the coeds. He was close, then closer, close enough to hear clearly as the runner shouted, "Rock-a-bye, baby/ Thy cradle is green/Father's a nobleman/ Mother's a queen."

What the hell? A nursery rhyme? He was concentrating so hard on reaching the guy that he almost missed seeing Gretchen stagger. She swung halfway around, a bewildered look on her face, took a step and crumpled to the ground.

"Gretchen!" he shouted.

The man in front of him cast a panicked glance over his shoulder and Kurt realized the guy hadn't known he was there. He was gaining on him, but the guy still reached Gretchen first, reaching down to get his hands on her arms and haul her to her feet. As he did, he spoke to her, although Kurt couldn't hear what he said.

But Gretchen was clearly still dazed and her body slumped, resisting his efforts. The man glanced at Kurt again, his eyes wild as he got Gretchen beneath the arms and tried to lift her again. She was becoming aware enough to recognize that something was awry and she began to struggle and scream, flailing at the hands grabbing her.

Kurt was almost there, almost near enough to get his hands on her abductor, but the man looked his way again. Apparently, he recognized the killing rage on Kurt's face because his expression changed, naked fear replacing alarm, and he immediately released Gretchen and ran.

Kurt was torn. Gretchen was on her hands and knees, and his first instinct was to go to her. He hesitated. She looked up at him and waved him on. "Go! Go get him!"

But the moment of hesitation had cost him. The

guy in the sweater reached a small foreign car parked across the street. There was someone in the driver's seat and the engine was idling, but the moment the man started across the street, the little car peeled out of the parking space. In the space of seconds, the guy wrenched open the door and dove into the passenger side as the car slowed. Then it picked up speed and rocketed away, squealing around a corner on two wheels.

Kurt stood at the edge of the street, panting heavily. He turned and looked back at Gretchen. There was a small crowd of students surrounding her and alarm bells clamoring in his head. There could be someone else in that crowd who intended her harm.

He reached her just as a young woman helped her to her feet. The man with her handed Gretchen her briefcase.

"Are you all right?" Kurt asked as he took her arm. "Thank you," he said, dismissing the students.

"I—I think so." She looked white and stunned.

The taxi driver hadn't left. He'd pulled his cab around the corner as he'd seen the drama unfold. "I saw the whole thing," he hollered across the top of the cab. "Shall I get a policeman?"

Police. "No, thanks," Kurt said. "I doubt they can catch him."

"Tried to get her bag, he did," said another student standing nearby.

Kurt lifted Gretchen and set her in the back seat

of the cab. "If you could just take us back to our hotel, that would be helpful," he said to the cabby. It was probably just as well the observers thought they had seen an aborted purse-snatching. He really couldn't imagine trying to explain any of the real story to local law officers. From his own years on the beat he knew that the wilder the story got, the deeper the officers' skepticism ran.

As the taxi pulled into traffic, the cell phone in his jacket rang.

"Kurt." It was Jake. "Are you with Gretchen?"

"Yes, but they almost got her."

Reaction set in and it must have resonated in his voice because Jake said, "Are you all right?"

"I will be, now that I know she's fine." He took a deep breath and steadied his shaking hands. "But we've got to get her someplace safe and keep her there for a while."

"You're right." Jake sounded shaken as well. "I'll meet you at the hotel and we'll figure something out."

Fourteen

Jake punched the off button on his cell phone and sat heavily on the edge of the bed in his hotel room. He cursed himself. He'd been so cautious about bodyguards and protection for himself ever since Zach's kidnapping, but it had never occurred to him to protect Gretchen until Kurt had noticed his own shadows.

He was still having a hard time reconciling the amazingly collected, quietly sweet Harvard professor with the hazy image of a laughing dark-haired sister named Grace. Perhaps that had affected his judgment. But he wouldn't be able to afford any more lapses like this one. The other siblings would have to be found and protected as soon as possible.

Thank God for Kurt Miller. Jake's self-disgust eased a little as he thought of the way the P.I. watched Gretchen, his eyes drinking in every move she made. Did she realize he loved her? There had been some sort of constraint between them last night, although it had largely disappeared by the time they'd finished talking at evening's end.

Thinking of his sister reminded him that he'd

promised to call Violet the moment he'd made contact with Grace. It had been too late last night. Flipping open his cell phone again, he dialed a series of numbers and waited.

"Hello?"

"Violet?" It still felt too strange to call someone other than his adoptive mother "Mom," but from the few details he could remember from his childhood, he'd called this woman that for most of his early years. Could he bring himself to call her that again? He wasn't sure, even though he knew the deliberate distance he kept between them hurt her. He felt bad about it, but he just wasn't ready for anything more. But one thing he was sure of—he'd seen the joy in her face when he'd acknowledged her place in his past, back in D.C., and he knew he could never consciously deprive her of a place in her children's lives again. He might not be able to call her Mom but she was part of his life now and she would stay a part of it.

He couldn't even imagine making the choices she'd been forced to make. Starting a whole new life after finding her husband murdered, giving up her own children so that they might escape the same fate—or a worse one.

"Jake!" Violet's voice grew animated. "Where are you?"

"London," he said. "I found Grace."

There was silence on the other end of the line.

"H-how is she?" His biological mother's voice was tentative. It almost sounded as if she were crying.

"She's fine now," he said, "but she was nearly kidnapped earlier this morning. I'm certain Croft was behind it. Grimble was posing as her birth father, trying to facilitate a meeting with her. When she refused, I guess they got desperate."

"Dear Lord." Violet was clearly shaken.

"Her name is Gretchen now. Dr. Gretchen Wagner." He said it partly to distract her from thoughts of a kidnapping. "She's a professor at Harvard. In fact, if you have this month's *National Geographic* lying around, read the article about the stone tablets being translated in Egypt. There are several photographs of her in it. You were right—she does look like you," he added as an afterthought.

"Is she…happy?" Violet asked.

His eyebrows rose as he considered his mother's question. "I think so," he said at last. "She seems to love her career. And she's got this guy—actually, he's a private investigator—who seems to be wild about her. He's the one who kept her from being snatched."

"Does she love him?"

Jake remembered the look in Violet's eyes as she had spoken of his father, Henry, when they'd met in D.C. He'd been the greatest love of her life. It made sense that she would want to see her own children find something as special. "I think she might," Jake said cautiously. "He certainly can't keep his eyes off her."

"Good," Violet said softly. "Good." Then, "I'd like to meet Gretchen and her private investigator."

Jake hesitated.

"What's wrong?" His mother's voice changed immediately, and he made a wry face. How had she figured out something was wrong just from a heartbeat of silence?

"I think we need to find a safe place to relocate my siblings as we find them," he said. "We could have lost her this morning if Kurt hadn't been there. I've had security with me since April, but it's not practical to attempt to keep everyone covered wherever they may be. I think that everyone, including you, should gather in one safe spot."

"Do you have any place in mind?"

"Not yet." He was truthful.

"What about your place in Texas?"

"Too public," he said promptly. "The media would be broadcasting my visitors' names and occupations and speculating about their extended presence. It would be like putting them all on display and saying, 'Here they are, come and get them.' Not to mention the fact that any group of people adopted as teens, all of whom have extraordinary abilities of some kind, would immediately be suspected to be the genetically engineered products of the Code Proteus experiment."

"You're right." He heard her sigh.

"What about your ranch in Colorado?"

"No," she said immediately. "If Croft is looking for me, he eventually may be able to trace me here. And it's so isolated we could be easily surrounded. This wouldn't be a safe location, either."

"All right," he said slowly. "I'll have to work on it. I'll let you know when I come up with something. In the meantime, tell me anything more you can remember about the process by which our memories were altered."

"I don't know much. The first time I realized it had occurred, I had been drugged and separated from you. I got away and stole you back, but you didn't even recognize me. I had to give each of you a tranquilizer, then move you one by one to my vehicle. That's when I was nearly stopped and Gideon—" her voice broke "—was shot. After that, I took you to an old friend whom your father and I trusted. He was a psychologist who knew a great deal about post-hypnotic suggestion, and while he wasn't able to undo whatever they had done to you, he managed to calm you enough that you accepted my guidance." She sighed. "That's really all I can tell you. After all this time, you still don't remember anything?"

"Little things have been coming back, but nothing significant. Gretchen's had a similar experience."

"I wonder if that's happening to the others. After all those reports about mutant children—" her voice registered her distaste for the term "—Faith and Mark may be curious about their early lives."

"Possibly. We've got to find them."

"If I think of anything new that could help, I'll call," Violet said.

"I've been working on locating people who fit their profiles," he said. "But it's going to take some time."

"I'm afraid we don't *have* a lot of time." Her voice shook. "Not after what they've already made Gideon do."

"We need more information." He was really talking to himself as much as to her. "I have an old buddy from college who's inside the White House now. I'm going to approach him, see if there's any way he can help me find out more about Medusa and the Code Proteus project."

"Please be careful," Violet pleaded. "You could be in terrible danger if they realize you're pursuing them. If they can't get to you and force you to cooperate, they may decide to eliminate you the way they did your father."

"I'll be cautious," he promised grimly. "And you do the same. As the only living person outside the group who knows everything about what occurred, you represent the most likely source of danger to the group."

"I know," she said. "I'm taking precautions. And we need to meet again soon. I have something very important to give you."

"What?"

"I'd rather not discuss it over the phone," she hedged.

"I'll call as soon as I'm back in the States and we'll arrange a time to get together," he promised. He glanced at his watch. "I'd better go. I'm meeting Gretchen and Kurt to brainstorm about where we could set up a secure base for everyone."

"All right." She hesitated. "Jake, I love you. Be careful."

He hesitated. "Thank you." The words were stupid and inadequate, but dammit, he couldn't help the way he felt. "See you soon."

Jake met them in Kurt's hotel room.

The moment the door closed, he walked to his sister and took her hands. It looked almost as if he wanted to embrace her, but couldn't quite bring himself to initiate the motion. Gretchen was too shocked to notice or respond. "Thank God you're safe." Jake looked up again, over her head at Kurt. "Thank you."

Kurt nodded. He was still pretty shaken himself. "It was dumb luck," he said. "I went into the hotel lobby and saw Gam—Grimble. I listened in on a phone conversation and when I realized he was talking to someone who was about to grab her, I got out of there."

Gretchen turned as Jake released her and put her hands up to Kurt's cheeks in a familiar motion he cherished. "You made it in time," she said. "That's what counts."

"Tell me exactly what happened." Jake began pacing the far end of the room.

Kurt relayed the sequence of events that he'd observed, and then Gretchen added her own comments about her assailant. "He said something to me," she said, frowning. "I can't remember what it was but it made me feel…powerless."

"It was a nursery rhyme," Kurt told her.

She looked blank. "I don't remember anything about a nursery rhyme. He said, 'Get up and get in the car.'"

"But before that, he quoted a nursery rhyme," Kurt said.

"Post-hypnotic suggestion," Jake said. "I believe they used nursery rhymes to program us. I remembered mine recently." He looked at Gretchen. "Any time you hear yours, it will act as a trigger to make you follow whatever directions you're given."

"But she didn't," Kurt said. "At first she responded but she started to struggle after a moment or two."

Jake's eyebrows rose. "That's a good sign. Maybe the rhymes' effects wear off if they aren't reinforced occasionally." He frowned. "I wish we knew the nursery rhyme. Then we could work on deprogramming you."

Kurt slipped a piece of paper from his pocket and handed it to Jake. "I wrote it down."

Jake looked pleased. "Thanks."

"Let me see that." Gretchen reached for the paper.

"No!" Both men spoke together.

"If it is a cue," Kurt said, "I don't want you seeing or hearing it ever again."

Gretchen made a face, but then she sighed. "You could be right." She eyed the piece of paper Jake was folding and placing in his wallet. "The thought that a few words could turn me into a zombie is scary."

"But you didn't do what you were told," Kurt reminded her. He felt almost sick when he recalled the way she'd dropped to the ground. He'd thought for a moment she'd been shot.

Her brow furrowed as she concentrated. "I didn't want to. Part of me felt as though I should, but I really didn't want to. And when I saw you running toward me, I knew I shouldn't get in that car. I couldn't make myself run away, but I was able to resist."

Jake was nodding again. "Hypnoses isn't as all-powerful as people think. A person can't be made to do something against his will with a post-hypnotic suggestion."

"Meaning?" Kurt lowered himself to the bed and pulled Gretchen into his lap. After what had happened earlier, he wasn't sure he was ever going to let her out of his reach again.

"The people hunting us implanted a suggestion that she would obey directions after she heard that nursery rhyme. It acted as a prompt. Except that Gretchen recognized that getting into that car was a bad idea, so she wouldn't do it."

"Thank God." Kurt buried his face in her hair.

Gretchen looked at her twin. "Am I going to have to live with that for the rest of my life?"

"I doubt it," Jake said. "If Maisy can't help us, I'm sure she knows other specialists we can consult."

"You think you have one of those prompts, too?" Kurt's eyebrows rose.

"I know I do," Jake said, frowning. "When they kidnapped my adoptive brother Zach, they tried to use it on him."

"If all five of you have these triggers," Kurt said slowly, "these people may believe they can control your actions once they get their hands on you."

"At least, they may have believed that until today," Gretchen said wryly. "Now, who knows?"

"I had a conversation with Vi earlier," Jake said. "She says the reason we can't remember our early life is because the memories were suppressed by Grimble and his cohorts. So we can probably consult the same person about both the prompts and the missing memories."

Gretchen's eyes grew bright and aware. "Do you really believe we might be able to get our memories back?"

Jake shrugged. "I wouldn't bet the farm, but it's a possibility. Now," he said firmly, "we have a much more immediate problem."

"What?" Kurt felt himself tense.

"Relax," said Jake. "I didn't mean danger was lurking outside the door."

"After what happened this morning, I wouldn't be surprised if it was." He was dead serious.

"And that's why we need to find a safe location for Gretchen until this is all over. Violet can join her there, and when we locate the others, they could stay there as well."

"What about you? You're a target, too," she said.

Jake spread his hands. "I have bodyguards with me now, and I'm working with the FBI. One of us has to deal with them if we want to share information, and since I'm already involved, there's no need to expose the rest of you."

"But this could take years," Gretchen protested. "You can't protect yourself every minute."

"We really don't have a choice." Jake crossed his arms, the discussion of his safety clearly over. "I hope it won't take that long, but certainly we won't get these guys overnight. So it needs to be somewhere that you can make a home, somewhere from which you can work."

Gretchen looked at him expectantly.

"But I don't have any great ideas," he said immediately. "My place in Texas is a media magnet, and Violet's home, which is in Colorado, is dangerous in a different way."

"Different how?" Kurt's mind was churning, flipping through places he'd been and discarding most of them as fast as they occurred to him.

"It's in the middle of nowhere," said Jake, "but it isn't particularly hard to get to. Someone with enough backup could block the exit routes and take anyone who's there."

"And since the World Bank Heist padded their pockets," Kurt said, "we can be sure manpower won't be a problem for them."

"Right." Jake fell silent. He turned to the window and brushed aside the curtain just far enough to allow him to stare at the scene outside.

For long minutes no one spoke. Gretchen had laid her head on Kurt's shoulder, and her arms were loosely linked around his waist. He cradled her in his lap, his cheek against her soft hair.

God, he'd almost lost her today. Every time he thought about it, he felt shaky inside all over again. He tightened his arms around her, feeling desperate. There *had* to be a safe place—

There was!

"Brunhia," he said aloud.

"What?" Jake turned from the window as Gretchen lifted her head so that she could see his face.

"It's not a what, it's a place." The more he thought about it, the better a solution it seemed and he couldn't get the words out fast enough. "I own most of an island three miles off the south coast of Portugal. There's absolutely nothing there but two small fishing villages near the island's only harbor. That's the only way in, the only way out. The rest of it is heavily wooded and completely inaccessible because of tricky sandbars and submerged rocks. Even the beaches are nothing but rock, and the only way to get there is to pay the local folks to take you through the channels surrounding the harbor when the tide is in. When it's out, there's no getting there at all unless you're a bird."

"Could we build there?" He could see Jake considering the idea.

"That's the beauty of it." Kurt grinned. "My uncle, from whom I inherited this white elephant, built a place there years ago when he discovered marble on the island. After the marble was played out, he lived there until he died. The house has six bedrooms and is reasonably well equipped."

"And we could outfit it with satellite access to the outside," Jake said, clearly enthusiastic. "We'd need to add a security system and the latest computer technologies—"

"And upgrade the generator if you want any of that to work," Kurt said wryly.

"Sounds too perfect to be true." The tension on Jake's face had eased visibly.

"It's far from perfect, but it's definitely true. The only hitch is that a friend of mine is staying there right now and I won't ask him to go elsewhere. He…needs the solitude."

"Could he be trusted?"

Kurt thought about Max Strong. "Yes. I believe he could."

"And you're sure you wouldn't mind us barging in for what could be a long-term stay?"

Kurt shook his head, smiling down at Gretchen in his arms. "Not at all."

The minute the door closed behind Jake, Kurt took Gretchen's chin in his hand and lifted her face to his. Setting his lips on hers, he kissed her with all the relief and love and need he'd been feeling since he'd seen that guy running at her.

Her arms tightened around him. "I love you," she murmured. "Thank you for coming after me this morning."

Kurt shook his head. "No thanks are necessary. I wasn't about to let anyone take you away from me."

"Tell me about Brunhia." She laid her head on his shoulder, face turned in toward his neck.

"It's beautiful, but it's very isolated. I hope you won't get too lonely."

"Will you be there?" It was a rhetorical question. She wrapped her arms around his neck and draped herself against him.

He cuddled her closer. "You bet."

"How close is the nearest obstetrician?"

He went rigid. "Why? Are you— You can't possibly know yet. Can you?" he demanded.

"No," she smiled at his shock. "Not for sure. But

our timing was extraordinarily good, so it's very possible."

"Yeah!" It was a deep, satisfied shout, an immediate primitive reaction that he didn't even question as he pumped a fist into the air. He wanted a child, not just any child, but one that he and Gretchen had made together, and the thought that she might very well be pregnant thrilled him beyond measure.

"And even if I'm not pregnant yet," she said, "it's bound to happen if we don't start taking precautions."

Kurt grinned. "The closest real doctor is on the mainland," he said. "But I think we can arrange some way to sneak in and out of Portugal for obstetric care if we have to."

"All right." She settled back against him again.

"There's one thing I think you're forgetting," he told her.

She looked genuinely mystified. "What?"

He picked up her left hand and took her fourth finger between his thumb and index finger, waggling it gently. "A ring. And a marriage license."

"Oh," she said faintly. "That would be...nice."

"If that's a yes, I'll take it."

She laughed, surging up against him for a kiss with completely un-Gretchen-like exuberance. "That's a yes!"

* * * * *

There are more secrets to reveal—
don't miss out!
Coming in August 2003 to
Silhouette Books

He thought it was a simple request, but when White House Advisor Matthew Tynan asked his trusted secretary, Carey Benton, to look into a defunct government program, he thrust them both into a world of intrigue, danger… and passion!

THE PLAYER
By
Evelyn Vaughn

Family Secrets: Five extraordinary siblings. One dangerous past. Unlimited potential.

And now, for a sneak peek,
just turn the page…

One

Matt wasn't sure when he'd started noticing. Three months ago? Six? But some mornings, Carey Benton was so pretty she was dangerous. Shiny brown hair. Smiling blue eyes. A wholesome, fresh face that belonged on the cover of *Seventeen* magazine more than it did inside the Beltway. She *was* too good to be true, yet there she sat, a sweet, dependable constant in his crazy life, and damned if she didn't brighten his mornings. And noontimes. And afternoons.

But no nights. If Matt wasn't so careful about workplace romances and younger women, he could easily screw up one of the best relationships he'd ever had.

His determination reinforced, he picked up the phone. "Talk to me, Jake. Are you postponing your wedding again?"

"Hey, Tynan." At the tension in his friend's voice, Matt forgot Carey—which was saying something. "I need a favor."

"Anything," Matt said. "You know that."

Jake Ingram *never* asked for favors. Hell, his old college buddy had so much more money than Matt, he'd never needed them. All Matt had was a way with women—and his job as a White House advisor.

"Anything that I can," he qualified.

"I need information—nothing that would compromise you," Jake hurried to add. "I'm hoping you can get details faster than I can. It has to do with an old CIA project—"

This didn't sound good. "CIA?"

"*Old* CIA," insisted Jake. "The project started almost forty years ago, and my information shows it was discontinued in the early '80s. With Freedom of Information, at least some of it should be declassified by now. But response time is a bear, especially with the red tape...."

"And you're hoping I can pull files from Pennsylvania Avenue faster than you can from Dallas." Matt drummed the end of a pencil on his desk. "I hate to disillusion you, pal, but I'm not sure even my boss has the power to speed up bureaucracy. Especially with those covert-op types."

"I know it's a long shot." Jake sounded like he used to during finals—short on sleep and pumped on challenge. "But there may be a connection between this project and the World Bank Heist."

"Whoa, there." Matt's pencil bounced off his desk. It had been two months since some techno-whiz called Achilles had hacked into the World Bank and transferred three hundred and fifty billion dollars into a series of dummy accounts and corporations. Matt knew that Jake had been hired to help the FBI investigate the crime. But—the *CIA?* "Connected with the W.B.H. how?"

"I can't tell you yet." At least Jake sounded truly regretful. "Hopefully once I've got more information, I can, but for now… It's just too dangerous."

"Yeah, you daredevil math guys like to ride the ragged edge." But Matt scrubbed a hand through his hair, concerned despite his joking. "I'll look into the matter, no problem. Would you mind if I put my assistant on it?"

"Carey? How much do you trust her?"

Matt considered the young woman on the other side of his closed door, ducked his head, and smiled. His admiration of her went far beyond appreciation of her shiny hair, welcoming eyes and willowy curves. He'd come to trust her more than his three-and-a-half mothers put together. "Implicitly."

"Then go for it. Um, Matt…" There Jake went, sounding furtive again. "I'll check back with you next week. But if you don't hear from me by that Friday, send the data to a woman named Gretchen Miller. Here's her number."

It was a foreign exchange. Matt didn't recognize the international calling code. "Got it." But Matt wasn't close to satisfied. "Is everything okay, Jake? Your brother's been all right since the kidnapping? Your parents?"

"My brother's in love," Jake said, as if that were any guarantee. "He's doing great. My family's fine."

Matt must have just imagined that his friend added, under his breath, "That one, anyway."